SURVIV🕱R MAX

Too Smart To Die

by
Davi Barker

NORTON PRESS

Just because the mind is blank
Doesn't mean the words are empty

About the Author

A lifelong connoisseur of the undead, Davi believes that art should imitate life, and if it can't, art should at least eat life's brain. Frustrated by the big lurkers and shakers in the zombie genre, Davi aims to redefine the quintessential metaphor of the living dead. Zombies are unique among monsters in that they outnumber the living, enacting one of literature's most enduring themes: the triumph of the individual over the collective. And as the masses return from the dead to consume the living, it is the survivors who build the new world from the corpse of the old.

Survivor Max: Too Smart To Die
ISBN: 978-1792668111
Copyleft ☺ 2018 by Norton Press

Printed on Earth (allegedly).

About Survivor Max

It started out as an alien story. An extraterrestrial on Earth in search of proof that humanity was ready to join the intergalactic community. There were thirteen kids from all over the world, but I kept getting stuck. What's a teenager's life like in China? Or Somalia? I was doing more research than actual writing.

Tarrin Lupo, author of <u>The Pirates of Savannah</u>, suggested that I had bitten off more than I could chew. That I shouldn't try to write an epic trilogy on my first try, and instead I should just finish one book about something I already knew well enough to write without all the research. I reduced the cast to one kid and replaced the aliens with zombies.

The next day, by coincidence or providence, I was on a plane seated next to a science teacher who was grading zombie stories written by kids Max's age. Many of Max's best ideas came from them. So the first book was dedicated to the 2015 graduating class of Thornton Central School.

When I started I folded and stapled by own chapbooks to hand out at festivals. My printing expenses were briefly sponsored by SurvivalGearBags.com, but ultimately Survivor Max was picked up by Prepper Press, a family-owned publishing house specializing in apocalyptic fiction and survival nonfiction. They wanted a book by that Christmas, but I was only a third done, so they offered me a three book deal, and published <u>Too Smart To Die</u> right away, and <u>School Bites</u> a year later.

<u>Trigger Warnings</u> was delayed over a year, first by my divorce, and then by the death of my mother. It's difficult to write about grief when you're going through it. Then the publisher decided to drop the third book. In the simplest terms, and the most convenient definitions, I imagine it was probably because the story was no longer the survival companion it began as (although that will always be part of the flavor). Max's story outgrew that box. Fans kept asking for it, and making suggestions, so in the age of self-publishing I decided that losing my publisher was no excuse not to continue.

Dedicated to the Thornton Central School
Graduating Class of 2015

One: Quarantined

The first rule of The Porcupine Scouts is, *LIVE! If you die, you've failed at survival.*

I was sitting in science class, and Ms. Lessard was writing "Active & Hidden" on the board. She began her lesson, "An active virus attacks healthy cells and hijacks them to spread itself. Active viruses present symptoms immediately, making them relatively easy to diagnose, and hopefully treat."

Science is my favorite subject. It is probably the only thing I like about school. But viruses are so kids' stuff for me. My dad is a scientist and talks about them all the time, so I was struggling to pay attention.

She continued, "Examples of active viruses are things like influenza, the mumps, and measles." She wrote them on the board. I doodled in my notebook. I was so bored.

She went on, "A hidden virus invades healthy cells, but allows them to function normally, so it spreads when the cells replicate. Hidden viruses lay dormant and don't express symptoms until the body is weak, making them harder to identify."

My phone made the signature jingle of a text message from Dad. I held the phone in my lap under the desk as I read, "They won't let me take you. The school is under quarantine. Get home now! Whatever it takes. I'll explain later."

I blinked. Quarantine? I looked out the window, where I could see the parking lot in the front of the school. Two ambulances had pulled up to the school, followed by the local police department's armored vehicle. Behind them was a huge black van that looked like some kind of mobile command center. It was from the New Hampshire Department of Health and Human Services. Strange. Very strange.

"Who can give me an example of a hidden virus ... Max?"

My attention darted from the window to the front of the room. The class snickered. It was one of those *gotcha* questions she only asked when she knew someone wasn't paying attention. I stared up at her blankly.

"Max, you know you're not supposed to be on your phone in class. Put it away, or I'm going to take it."

I put the phone in my pocket. "Sorry," I said. Then the school's lockdown alarm went off and the class erupted in panicked gasps.

"Calm down everyone! It's probably only a drill." Ms. Lessard began closing the window blinds, pausing when she saw the scene in front of the school. She continued with a slight quiver in her voice. "Everyone get under your desks. Max, would you lock the door?"

I stood up, but hesitated before going to the door. I looked at my phone again. "Whatever it takes." I grabbed my book bag and ran out.

As I ran through the halls I tried to call Dad, but he wasn't picking up. Principal Bownes came on the loudspeaker. "Governor Warden has announced a state of emergency in Thornton, and all of Grafton County. Everyone stay calm. Teachers, please bring your classes to the auditorium in an orderly fashion for roll call. Parents have been called. Everything is under control."

They called our parents, but wouldn't let them take us? That made no sense. Classroom doors were flung open and students poured into the hall. Teachers tried to keep them together but it was chaos.

I stepped out of the green steel doors at the front of the school, and bumped right into the school resource officer, a dim witted giant named Pike.

"Hey! Get to the auditorium!" He put one hand on my shoulder and the other on his Taser as he began pushing me back inside.

He's pretty slow, not just mentally, but physically, too. So, I considered running past him, but the heavily armed officers in head-to-toe body armor who were filling up the parking lot behind him made me reconsider. So, I tried something else.

Despite his uniform, and his badge, Pike was the dumbest member of the faculty. Sure, security was his job, but breaching security was as easy as outsmarting him.

I faked up a nasty sounding cough, and sniffled as I rubbed my nose across my arm. "Principal Bownes told me to go to the nurse's office and wait. I guess I got a little turned around. I'm feeling really light headed."

His eyes went wide and he quickly took his hand off my shoulder and rubbed it on his black pants.

He pointed toward the nurse's office, and told me to wait there even though it was already evacuated. Once he was gone I slipped out a window.

Behind the school there was the playground, behind that, a field, and behind that open wilderness. At the far end, I saw two men in city jumpsuits constructing a chain-link fence across the back of the school yard. As soon as they saw me we all began running toward the opening in the fence.

I barely made it through ahead of them. I heard one yell after me, "Hey kid! Come back!" The other yelled, "You'll be sorry you left."

They didn't chase, and I escaped into the woods. I didn't know what the lockdown was for, but I knew a quarantine was to prevent the spread of disease. That was Dad's area of expertise. I figured I'd get all the answers when he got home from work.

Two: Home Sweet Home

My name is Max. I'm eleven years old, and a bit small for my age. I am no good at sports, but I love science. I like to figure out how things work, and make them work better.

I knew my way through the woods. I had been trained for that. I had about twenty pounds of books strapped to my back, but my favorite was my Porcupine Scouts Survival Guide. PorcScouts is a tight-knit group of families who go on outdoor adventures, share campfire stories and learn wilderness survival. I like it because it is science in action. Some physics, some biology, occasionally some chemistry, but always with a practical application. Not the abstract book learning in school.

It was a three mile walk to get home by street, but I avoided the main road by crossing directly through the woods. Once I got to my street I took a footpath along the creek, on the other side of the tree line. I could still see the road, but I didn't want anyone to see me. Dad's text was confusing, and he still wasn't responding. I was worried someone bmighte looking for me.

The cool autumn air and the sounds of the forest were soothing after my daring escape from the school lockdown. In town nature was drowned out by the sound of cars and people, but the forest was filled with songbirds and the sweet orange smell of sugar maples. Seed pods from sugar maple trees have wings that make them spin like a helicopter when they fall. I tried to pluck them out of the air as I walked.

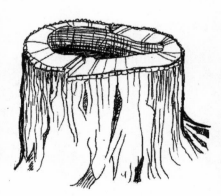

I live with my dad in a gated community called Lochshire Estates. It's a new development, pretty much a walled compound. As I approached, I took all the seed pods I'd caught and dumped them in a hollowed out stump outside the compound. I did this whenever I walked through the woods, hoping that one of them would germinate and someday I'd get to see a tree growing inside another tree.

There was a delivery truck from the post office parked in front of the compound. The Postman was filling his bag with mail for the residents of Lochshire.

"Do you have anything for unit 4D?" I asked.

He frowned at me and brushed me away. "Leave me alone, kid. You'll get your mail when I'm good and ready to give it to you."

I was a stunned by his rudeness, but didn't let it bother me. I swiped an electronic keycard and walked through the entry gate of the compound.

"Hey, Sam. What's the good news?"

Sam was the security guard at the front gate. He was more of a toll booth operator really, except there was no toll. On a typical day we talked, usually about the news. I liked him. He was funny. But this time he didn't even look up from his mini TV. He just waved me through. It was unusual. From the flashes on the screen it looked like the Black Friday rush at Lincoln Square Shopping Center just north of here, but Christmas is months away. Maybe it was a riot, but why riot in a little town like Lincoln, New Hampshire? I walked through.

There are six apartment buildings in the compound. Three of them are two-story red buildings we call "the bricks." The other three are four-story buildings we call "the towers." They aren't towers in any conventional sense, but in a little town like Thornton, buildings don't get much taller than four stories. We lived on the top floor of the east tower.

I went through the lobby and walked toward the elevator. I pushed the button and watched as the needle rattled on the second floor. *Rats!* This happened when something was blocking the door. It just opened and closed over and over. I headed for the closest stairwell.

A stranger I'd never seen before was at the far end of the hall, at the entrance to the other stairwell. He was old, dressed in a gray corduroy jacket and bow tie, but his clothes were all torn and stained. He looked like I imagined hobos look, except that I'd never actually seen a hobo. He was knocking on the door to the stairwell, which was weird enough because it wasn't locked, but he even did it in a strange way. His knees were locked and his chest and face were pressed up against the door like someone being arrested. He was smacking his palms against the door in a slow, steady thud, like fish slapping on a deli counter.

8

I watched the man, confused by how he was acting, when he finally noticed me. I couldn't say for sure, but it seemed like he smelled me, taking in a long breath through his nose as he turned his head and looked right at me. His eyes were glassy, and his face was pale. He sent me a cold stare that gave me the creeps, but I was not going to wait around to find out why. I shot up the stairs to the fourth floor, swiped my electronic key to our apartment and went inside.

Something was wrong.

The dining room table was turned on its side. Magazines, pens, and mail were all over the floor. The shelf in the living room was face down on a pile of books and DVDs. The sliding glass door to the balcony was wide open and the curtains were torn down.

My heart began racing, but I stopped myself, and remembered the second rule of PorcScouts, *Don't Panic. What you know is more important than what you have.* I took a deep breath, and tried to imagine what a private investigator would do.

I went back to the door and examined the frame. There was no sign of forced entry. I retraced the path of destruction through the apartment, using my phone's camera to document the damage. I took great relief that there was no blood or signs of a fight. Dad probably wasn't home yet.

It didn't look like anything was stolen, just broken. In fact, common valuables were left in plain sight. I photographed the desktop computer, which had been smashed on the ground. Maybe it was just vandalism.

I tracked the damage from the kitchen, to the dining room, to the living room. I gulped when I saw Dad's wallet on the coffee table.

"Dad! Are you here?" I half yelled, my voice cracking. There was no answer.

I heard a siren in the distance and stepped out on the balcony to see if I could spot it. It sounded like it was right outside, but I couldn't see it. Then it faded away.

Suddenly I heard a strange, bone-chilling sound inside the apartment. It was a low, wet growl. Almost a gurgle, like a dinosaur with a mouth full of marbles. It turned my guts upside down. I was afraid to look, but I forced myself to turn, slowly peeking back through the torn curtains.

Dad was standing in the hallway to the master bedroom. At least it looked like Dad, but he had the same gray face as the stranger downstairs. He lurched into the living room, sniffed in my direction, and gave me the same foggy stare. I was trembling, but he didn't pause for a second. He crept toward me with slow, heavy foot falls, his fingers out in a grasping motion, his mouth open.

My brain was frozen, but my hands had a plan of their own. In an instant they threw the sliding glass door shut, and fumbled with the handle, but I couldn't lock it from the outside.

There was no way I could hold the door closed. He would overpower me, and force it open.

Dad, or whatever it was, built up speed and lumbered toward the balcony door, but he didn't go for the handle. Instead he smacked against the glass with full force, like a bird flying into a window. The impact made a long diagonal crack in the glass and the man began pounding and biting at it.

I fell back, watching as he tried to eat his way through. Why didn't he open the door? "Dad, what's wrong? It's me, Max!" He showed no sign of comprehending. He had only one goal, to get me, and then... I didn't even know. "Dad, stop! You're scaring me!" My face was wet with tears.

A second crack crossed the first. I was dead for sure. I came to my senses and backed up all the way to the railing, looking for something to defend myself. I looked over the edge, but the ground below was way too far to jump.

As he pressed harder, the glass began to give way. He came through head first, cutting up his own face. Whatever that thing was, it wasn't Dad. It wasn't even human.

In a flash, I had an idea! I roughly guessed the speed and force, the necessary leverage and distance. This could work. It had to! I spun a balcony chair between me and the creature, and I stood between the chair and the rail.

The glass crumbled away and the creature rushed at me, lunging over the chair to grab me. When it stepped on the extended foot of the chair,

I pushed down hard on the back, using the chair as a simple catapult. The front shot up, lifting the attacker off its feet and launching it over the railing.

I turned and grabbed the railing, my knuckles white, and watched the creature spinning off the fourth story balcony. Its body crashed against the asphalt, broken but twitching. What was it? It had Dad's hair, and it wore Dad's clothes, but it wasn't Dad. Was it? My whole body was shaking. I felt the blood rush out of my face, and thought I might be sick. Did I just kill my dad?

Three: No Escape

My heart was pounding. My chest heaved. Panic overtook me.
I ran screaming from the apartment. The elevator was still stuck, so I
charged down the stairs at full speed. I made the first turn toward the
third floor when my heart, my breath, and my feet all came to a skidding
halt, and I was face-to-face with the stranger from first floor. It had
followed me up the stairs, and now we were locked eye-to-eye. Its
pupils were as tight as pin pricks.

The stranger snarled up at me. A gust of hot putrid smelling breath hit
me in the face. It was like a broccoli tuna casserole that was overcooked
and left in the sun until the mayonnaise went bad. I nearly barfed right
then and there, but the creature grabbed my legs. No time to puke. I
kicked and scrambled backwards up the stairs.

It didn't give much of a chase. It limped and dragged its feet up each
step. Its legs were twitching chaotically as it made the climb.

I ran back to my door, fumbled for my card and swiped it. I looked back
at the intruder stumbling out of the stairwell and into the hall. It
spotted me, and charged. It could move pretty fast in a straightaway. I
slammed the door just as it crashed against the door with 180 pounds of

dead weight. The door popped open a few inches, but I slammed my shoulder back against it and just managed to snap the deadbolt in place.

Phew!

It began pounding on the door, snarling and scratching. I pushed the coffee table in front of the door and huddled in the farthest corner of my bedroom. I tucked my knees against my chest, and covered my ears with my hands, repeating, "This isn't real, this isn't real, this isn't real," over and over to drown out the sound. After a few hours, the pounding outside slowed into a rhythmic thump. Eventually even that went silent, and I fell asleep.

I woke up early the next morning to the sound of screaming, and looked out my bedroom window. The parking lot was full of people trying to escape. Some were running on foot with their families while others were franticly loading up their vehicles. Everyone had paused and was looking toward the source of the yelling, a male voice.

The screaming man was on the ground, wrestling with a woman in a red sweater. He put his hand over her face and pushed her away when she grabbed his arm with both hands and bit into the meat of his palm.

It was one of them. It must be contagious.

His screams echoed throughout the compound, but they petered out into a gurgle as the woman overpowered him. I couldn't see very clearly because there was a half-loaded station wagon in the way, but everyone who could see watched in horrified silence.

The silence was broken by the sobbing of a young boy in the back of the station wagon. The creature immediately released its victim and lunged for the boy. He slammed the car door shut, but the creature's fingers wedged in the door, preventing it from latching. It forced the door open and dove in after him.

The crowd freaked, abandoned their vehicles, and ran screaming for the front gate.

I still felt sick, but I forced myself to go to the balcony and look over the edge. Dad was still at the bottom; its legs were completely crushed from the fall. Its belly was torn open. At first I thought it was strange that no one had called an ambulance, but then that was no typical morning, and the ambulances were probably busy elsewhere.

Dad wasn't dead. It reached for me when it saw me, raising its arms into the air. I could still hear it growling. Was that thing my dad? I couldn't comprehend it. Why didn't it die?

Two more creatures were shambling toward the building. They probably heard the yelling. One of them caught its toe on a speed bump and fell flat on its face. I cringed when I saw its teeth were smashed in, but it didn't seem to mind. It just continued its relentless crawl forward. I went inside to avoid stirring up any more attention.

They seemed to be attracted to sound. That was valuable to know. And they seemed really tough, but stupid, and clumsy. If they were brain dead, my mind was my biggest advantage.

I mustered the courage to step up on the coffee table by the door and peer out the peephole. The creature's face was pressed against the door. It wasn't sleeping. I could see its open eye rolling around in its skull. It was waiting.

I backed away quietly.

I went to the phone, but there was no signal. I turned on the TV and found the Emergency Broadcast Signal. I immediately muted the volume so the lamebrain in the hall didn't hear. It was on every channel. The emergency instructions scrolled across the bottom of the screen.

> "This is the Emergency Broadcast Signal. This is not a test. The Governor has declared a state of emergency throughout the State of New Hampshire. All residents are ordered to return to their homes or nearest places of safety and remain there until further notice. All roads and bridges are to remain clear for emergency personnel. Residents are advised to stay calm. Do not panic. Everything is under control."

What a joke. I couldn't leave the apartment even if I wanted to. I was trapped. The broadcast contained absolutely no useful information, and even worse, it was overriding all the news channels that might have told me what was really going on.

I needed more information, to know what I was up against. I went to the Internet.

The computer in the living room was smashed, but Dad had a zPad. Dad's room was more trashed than the living room. Drawers were pulled out of the dresser and thrown through the closet doors. Clothes were everywhere. The bed was turned up and leaning against the wall. Everything from the desk was littered all over the floor. I had to search the mess for the zPad. I booted it up when I found it, but I was quickly confronted by a password request.

I guessed a few times, but Dad was too smart to use something obvious. I clicked "forgot my password" and it gave me three security questions.

"What was your junior high school mascot?"

That was easy. Dad went to my school. I typed in "Tigers." Next.

"What are the last 5 digits of your driver's license number?"

I grabbed the wallet he left on the coffee table and rummaged through it. "31415." Next.

"Who is your favorite author?"

Now that was tricky. I tried some of the obvious answers. "Marshall Rosenberg." Access denied. "Dr. Mary Ruwart." Access denied. "Tarrin Lupo." Access denied.

I sat back, stumped. I began digging through the books scattered on the floor. Under the pile I spotted a broken picture frame, and picked it up. The glass was shattered, but it was a familiar photo of Dad holding me as a baby. Then I noticed a detail I'd never seen before. There was another hand on Dad's shoulder. I pulled the frame apart and the photograph inside was folded to hide a third person.

It was Mom.

Mom died when I was too young to remember. I'd only heard stories about her. I turned the photo over, and there was written, "Rich, Joy and Max at Roger's Campground." The handwriting was curvy. Probably hers.

Then I remembered that Mom was an author. She wrote a science fiction novel called *Psychoclass A* before I was born. I'd never read it.

16

I went back to the zPad and entered, "Joy Hartwell." *Success!* I was quickly greeted by the home screen of Dad's zPad and the unfinished draft of an email to the Centers for Disease Control.

> *Dr. Blum,*
>
> *I am the lead virologist for Fr33 Aid. We are a mutual aid organization that provides medical services and research on a voluntary basis. I'm attaching a file containing all my research on a strange epidemic we're seeing in New Hampshire. We've traced the outbreak to a Veteran's Administration Outpatient Clinic in Littleton, NH that was apparently conducting human trials of a vaccine from your agency.*
>
> *This outbreak is uniquely difficult to contain because there's actually two pathogens working together, reinforcing each other: one active, and one hidden.*

I thought back to science class.

> *The combination causes a horrific transformation with terrifying implications for your test subjects, and anyone they have come in contact with. We know the active infection is transmitted through bodily fluids, especially by bites. But we don't know how far the hidden infection has spread because it doesn't show any immediate symptoms. All we know is that it's airborne.*

I remembered the stench of the lamebrain in the hall.

> *The transformation is triggered by bites from someone with the active infection. But even without being bitten anyone with the hidden infection will still change after they die, even if it's from natural causes. Once the transformation is complete their body will reanimate. For patients who are alive at the time of infection, the transformation is violent and painful, resulting in explosive fits of hysteria and rage.*

I glanced around the room.

The infection attacks the brain, destroying the frontal cortex, crippling reason, language and memory. It erases the human part. Then it targets the fight or flight mechanism. It subdues fear, pain, and even survival reflexes, leaving only the instinct to hunt, attack and eat. What remains is a primitive mental state. All fight and no flight. The infected have been observed consuming animals, but their primary prey is us.

They do not negotiate. They do not retreat. They do not sleep. They do not __

The email ended abruptly with no signature. Dad had worked late every day that week, and stayed up late working from home. It was always something important when he got manic like that, but this was insane.

I pushed "send."

Four: Hunkered Down

I did a little poking around on the internet looking for more information, but as soon as I saw reports that power was shut off in Littleton, I stopped surfing and started printing a hard copy of Dad's research while I still could. It was about a hundred pages, but if things got really bad it might be the only copy left. It might be the only chance for a cure.

I remembered my PorcScouts training. The third rule of PorcScouts is, *Three minutes without air, three days without water or three weeks without food and you're dead.*

Priority number one was water. I filled the bathtub while the printer was running. My PorcScounts Survival Guide suggested one gallon per person per day; half to drink and half to use for cooking and cleaning. People think it's a good idea to ration drinking water and skimp on sanitation, but they're wrong. It increases the risk of more dangerous health issues. The guide also said the eight glasses of water per day suggestion was a myth. Thirst is the best gauge for water consumption. If you're thirsty, drink. Period. There's no reason to drink more than usual after a disaster.

I made some quick calculations. The bathtub was 24 inches wide, 60 inches long and 18 inches deep. Length, times width, times height gave me 15 cubic feet of water. Using the conversion of roughly 7.5 gallons per cubic foot, that was 112.5 gallons. It was probably less, because of the slope inside of the tub, but I would probably need a little less because I was small. There would be snow before I would run out of water, anyway.

Snow.

Cold was going to be a serious issue if this situation lasted long enough, especially with the balcony door broken. Winters in New Hampshire were dangerous. There were trees in the compound that I could chop if I had an ax. But chopping wood surrounded by hungry monsters that are attracted to sound was a stupid plan. I had time. I'd come up with something.

The next priority was food. I ran to Dad's closet where he kept some emergency food. There was a plastic bucket filled with 120 individually wrapped meal packs. They were dehydrated and vacuum sealed to last longer. There was chicken pasta, cheesy macaroni, beef lasagna and tomato soup packs. Food wasn't going to be a problem for more than a month.

Behind the bucket I found a basic 72-hour emergency kit. It had water purification tablets, a tube of waterproof matches, a three pack of green glow sticks, a compact emergency blanket, fifty feet of paracord, duct tape and a basic first aid kit. It was a good thing he was so well prepared for any crisis. I felt like he was still looking out for me.

Behind the emergency kit I found something I'd forgotten about, a handheld two-way radio, which reminded me of Dad's advice.

***

"If we ever get separated in an emergency these supplies are here for you, but if you have to leave without me, make sure to leave one of these radios here for me. That way we can communicate and I can find you." Dad handed me one radio and held the other in his hand.

I pushed a button on the radio, letting out a piercing shriek of feedback.

Here, let me show you" said Dad. He proceeded to explain to me the workings of the radio, which would allow us to communicate at great distances, even if the power and the phones were out.

I interrupted, "Why would we get separated?"

He explained, "We probably won't, but being prepared means always having a backup plan. This is our backup plan."

I nodded, sullenly.

"Don't worry, Max. I'm a survivor, and you're my son. That makes you a survivor. Besides, before you know it you'll be all grown up, and on your own, and I'll be the old man on the radio needing your help."

I laughed.

"Until then, I'm going to do everything in my power to make sure we never get separated in a crisis, but just in case, you need to know how to get to the cabin on your own."

"I understand."

***

I missed him, but I wasn't sad. I wasn't anything. I was just numb inside. It didn't even seem real.

The second radio was gone. Dad had been in the process of bugging out.

I had to get to the bug-out location by myself. The cabin was at Stinson Lake, about thirty miles away by road, but only ten miles if I went through the woods. The woods were probably safer anyway. The cabin was stocked with food, water, medicine, and even weapons, which were against the Lochshire housing agreement. Plus, the other PorcScouts families might go there, if they survive.

I ran to the balcony and looked out. Dad's survival gear bag was in the trunk of his car, which was parked near the south tower. It had all the gear I needed to go through the woods, but Dad had the keys. If I could get the keys, and get the bag, I could get to the cabin on foot. But first I had to figure out how to escape the apartment.

There was no way I was going to fight an adult lamebrain. I had to think of some other way out. I thought about trying the catapult again, but that would only work on the balcony. I'd have to let it chase me through the apartment. No. I had time to come up with something better.

I'd wait it out. I figured if it eats it must eventually starve, right? Humans, if it was even still human, can only survive three weeks without food, and only three days without water. I had a pantry full of food, a bathtub full of water, and the emergency supplies. I had time on my side.

Five: Talking Heads

I spent a few hours searching the Internet for information about the outbreak. Almost every news site was displaying a map provided by the Department of Homeland Security breaking the country into the color-coded terrorism threat levels. Most of the country was "elevated" (yellow). Everything east of the Appalachians was "high" (orange). New Hampshire was "severe" (red).

Reports of attacks came from as far south as Keene, but no reports came from further north than Littleton. Details were hard to come by.

Each new outbreak started in a local hospital. Emergency personnel brought the infected there for medical treatment, and then they changed while they were in the hospital and attacked. Video from Concord showed a mob of clumsy cannibals filling the streets. They devoured crowds of panicked people and overwhelmed police roadblocks. The worst part was that the infected didn't just kill. They converted their prey. So, even when emergency personnel thought they'd cleared an area, if even one lamebrain survived, it attacked the rescue team and the outbreak started all over.

The talking heads and news reporters were clueless. I heard a radio host blame the attacks on a new street drug called poX. He was screaming at a caller, a nasally woman who seriously thought the infection was a side effect of global warming. *Idiots!*

The worst part was the home videos. There were already dozens of viral videos posted with the hashtag *#bitergram*. And it wasn't just recorded attacks. I found a video of teenagers laughing and throwing rocks at a lamebrain that got stuck in wet concrete. In another video, someone hung a lamebrain in a tree with a noose and people stood around and beat it like a piñata. It was disgusting.

I wanted science, and I finally found it in a video of this internet show called *Info Planet* with Joel Saxen. He was a pirate radio broadcaster from somewhere in New Hampshire. No one knew where his studio was, but he posted the video feed from his webcam.

***

The show began with intro music that sounded like Beethoven's *Funeral March* played with bagpipes and bombs dropping, then the announcer's voice interrupted, "Live, waging his crusade on ignorance. It's Joel Saxen, broadcasting to you via satellite from the *Info Planet*."

Joel was sitting in front of a microphone in a studio with two darkened video feeds superimposed along the bottom of the screen. "Guys and gals, this your host Joel Saxen, and today we're going to cut right to the root because I have a very special show planned for you. No one is covering this. The public is being lied to. Go to my website, the documents are there. The cult of government has been preparing for this plague for years. Militarizing the police. Secret funding for biological research. The new continuity of government procedures that changed ONE WEEK before the outbreak."

He slammed his fist on the desk and actually made the video feed flicker, startling himself.

"Folks, I've got two guests on the line with me who are going to tell us what we're up against. I've got Dr. Blum, a virologist from the Centers for Disease Control in Atlanta, Georgia."

That's the guy Dad was writing to. The left video feed lit up revealing a friendly looking bald guy in reading glasses and v-neck sweater.

"And Dr. Murphy, a professional neurobiologist with a PhD from Dartmouth, here in New Hampshire." The right video feed revealed a grinning younger woman with dark curls and a white lab coat. "Welcome aboard the *Info Planet*. What can you guys tell me?"

Dr. Blum began. "What we know for sure is that it's in the blood. It could be a virus, a bacteria, a parasite, or possibly a fungus. We don't know for sure, but given how rapid the infection takes over, we believe that indicates a virus. Probably an extremely virulent strain of rabies. But that's good news, because it means a vaccine is definitely possible, and the CDC is working on it."

Dr. Murphy interrupted. Her voice was smooth and inviting. "I recognize the need to believe that a vaccine is coming, but we can't let that desire cloud our judgment. With all respect I think you're way off. No virus can cause what we're seeing. We're not just talking about dementia, or fever. This is rapid mental, physical and behavioral changes. This thing hijacks the whole brain. We're looking at a highly infectious human strain of mad cow disease. It explains the jerky movement, the aggression, the loss of speech and memory.

23

"Wait, isn't mad cow disease a virus?" asked Joel.

"No. It's a protein infection called a *prion*. A mutated protein that replicates by converting neighboring proteins, causing degenerative brain damage, which is not treatable, and universally fatal."

Dr. Blum looked upset. "You're forgetting that mad cow disease is spread by eating tainted meat, not by tainted meat eating you.

Joel interrupted, "Hey, let's have a little respect. We're still talking about people's friends and loved ones. Let's refrain from referring to people as tainted meat.

"I apologize."

Joel continued, "What steps do you recommend people take to protect themselves?"

Dr. Blum began, "Well, we believe the hysteria is far more dangerous than the disease itself. The police and military are doing all they can to contain the infection. Yet, we're seeing waves of looting and violence in unaffected areas. We're advising people to stay calm and trust the government in their area. Everything is under control. If you're really worried, take this opportunity to assemble an emergency kit with enough food, water and supplies for at least seventy-two hours. But honestly, I think we're seeing a huge overreaction."

"What say you, Dr. Murphy." quipped Joel.

"Well, I agree we should keep calm. Our reason is our greatest advantage over this disease. As for the rest, I could not disagree more. I think we are looking at a pandemic of continental, perhaps global, proportion. My advice is that survivors do not engage infected people. Quarantine them if possible, avoid any contact until we know more. Until then it is utterly crucial that everyone be ready to defend themselves if the time comes. It's going to get a lot worse before it gets better."

Joel continued. "Some people have suggested that it's safer up north, that the cold slows them down, maybe even freezes them. What do you guys think?"

Dr. Blum bristled, "All we hear is more fear mongering. Even if it's true, that's no reason to act rashly. The infection hasn't even spread out of

New Hampshire. No one official has ordered any kind of northern exodus. Our best advice is to follow the orders of your local authorities."

Dr. Murphy had a look of confused disbelief. "Joel, I am willfully defying the governor's orders to evacuate my lab, but I am not moving north, either. This is where I am needed. This is where I can do the most good. I'm staying right here in Keene, New Hampshire. If the winter months offer me some added protection I'll be sure to let you know, but I know this for sure, 'just following orders' has gotten far too many people killed in the last century. No one has all the answers. People should assess their situation independently and do whatever they feel is best for their family."

Joel interrupted the arguing scientists. "Guys, isn't it possible that what we're seeing has been genetically engineered by the globalists to terrify the population into accepting another dramatic power grab by the government?"

Both scientists gave him the funniest looks of confusion and disbelief and then answered in unison, "No."

The exit music began, signaling the end of the segment. Joel concluded by saying, "You heard it here first. This plague is nothing more than the latest attempt by international elites to justify their agenda of forced vaccinations, socialist death panels, and population control on the entire planet by a hegemonic one world government. Stick around for more after this message from Aquarius Tactical Water Purifiers."

***

I turned it off. Dad's email said it was airborne.

Six: Stir Crazy

Deciding to wait for the lamebrain to starve meant having lots and lots of time on my hands. I tried to read Dad's research to pass the time.

> *Rapid testing of initially reactive skin tissue has proven problematic. The moment samples are taken, infected cells begin self-digesting, distorting the results. All 19 test samples became necrotic within 48 hours. This will make it difficult to screen for infection outside the lab. A rapid test kit suitable for field teams has proven impossible, regardless of initial tissue quality.*

I skipped ahead.

> *Infected brain tissue is covered in microscopic holes, like a sponge. Clinical signs include dementia, sound sensitivity, and extreme aggression. Subjects exhibit muscle twitching, pupil contraction and insomnia. These symptoms could form the basis for a diagnosis, except that peer research all suffers from a childish obsession with the 'spooky' symptoms, which have little diagnostic significance. As a result, they're calling the disease 'ataxic hyperphagia' or 'Walking Hunger.' I grudgingly accept this nomenclature as long as the diagnostic importance of spongiform brain damage is not overlooked.*

Everything else may as well have been in Chinese. It was pages of technical language, charts and graphs of numbers I didn't understand. I looked up "ataxic hyperphagia" online. "Ataxia" is a jerky, unbalanced walking style due to loss of muscle control. "Hyperphagia" means insatiable hunger, or compulsive eating. *Walking Hunger.* Creepy.

I occupied myself by watching news and other viral videos. Experts said lamebrains could only be "dispatched" by destroying the brain. You could stab them, shoot them, or even burn them. It didn't matter. If they still had a brain they would keep coming with whatever strength they had left.

As time went on, people got more creative with their #bitergram videos. A man tied up his wife and performed some kind of exorcism. Unsuccessfully, I might add. In another video, a couple of guys chopped off a lamebrain's feet and made it chase them through some kind of obstacle course. People can be sick. It made me wonder if becoming a lamebrain wasn't an improvement in some cases.

Thornton police promised to protect anyone who reached the refugee center at my school. Then it was overrun. After that, the governor announced that there was a heavily defended FEMA camp in Manchester. It was overrun, too.

In one video, a panicked army major cried in confused desperation, "We held the wall. They came from inside the green zone. How'd they get in there? We held the wall!" They didn't know about the hidden virus. They only knew about the active virus. It was obvious to me what had happened. The government promised protection to any survivors who could reach the base. Then they let in healthy looking people who had the hidden virus. It was just a matter of time until someone died inside and came back as a lamebrain.

Concentrating people was a bad idea. Cities were hit the worst. Soon every major city in New England was fighting the Walking Hungry.

After three days, I started checking on the lamebrain in the hall every morning, and every morning it was still standing there waiting. By the time the power went out it was clear the thing wasn't going to die from lack of water.

I remembered PorcScouts Rule #34, *In the event of a blackout eat all the ice cream.* It really meant eat anything frozen, since it was going to melt anyway. No sense in letting it go to waste. We had a pint that was homemade by one of the PorcScouts moms. The flavor was something she called, "Bananarchy." Dad always said that when I grew up I could eat as much ice cream as I wanted. I guess it was time to grow up.

There was also some frozen venison in the freezer, and some vegetables in the refrigerator that would go bad before long. I knew it would be the last real quality meat I'd have for a long time, so I decided to make a real feast out of it.

A blackout also meant no stove, no oven, and no central heat. So, it was time to build a fire. Building a fire indoors with no fireplace was against everything I'd ever learned about fire safety, but what choice did I have? Dad used to say, "The reason to learn the rules is so you know when to break them."

I started by clearing everything flammable away from the center of the living room, and built a makeshift barbeque. I put a broiling pan in the center of the room to protect the floor. On top of that I placed a cast iron Dutch oven to house the flame, and on top of that I placed the rack out of the oven. It would work if I was careful.

I grabbed my PorcScouts Survival Guide for fire building instructions.

> *Building a fire requires five essential parts: tinder, kindling, fuel, water and a fire starter. Tinder is any small dry twigs or leaves. Paper works perfectly well. Anything that will burn easily. Place your tinder in the center of your fire pit.*

I used all the old mail and newspapers that were strewn around on the floor. I ripped them into strips and crumpled them into a loose ball. Then I placed the ball in the Dutch oven.

> *Kindling is any small sticks or thin branches. Kindling must also be completely dry. Stack your kindling on top of the tinder in a 'teepee' structure, making sure to leave access to the tinder underneath. This is a fire-ready structure. You can start your fire by lighting the tinder with your fire starter.*

I had to be a little more creative to come up with kindling. I didn't exactly have a lot of twigs and branches laying around. I decided to use my school books, specifically History, Civics, and Economics. I used a match from the emergency kit to light the kindling and blew on it gently until it glowed with a hot orange light, and pages of the text books began to blacken and burn.

> *Once the kindling has caught, you can begin adding fuel. Fuel is any larger, denser wood that will take longer to light, and longer to burn. You can build this as large as you want, and the structure is less important, but be careful. It's important to have water on hand to put the fire out when the time comes.*

I didn't have the water to spare, but I did have a fire extinguisher. I had to keep the fire relatively low and controlled, so for fuel I pulled the faces off the drawers in the kitchen. It was a small fire, but on a cold night it would make all the difference.

I didn't really know how to cook a steak, so I just put it on the grill frozen and covered it in barbeque sauce. It was obvious pretty quickly that it wasn't going to work, so I chopped it into pieces. The milk and cheese were going to go bad, too, so I decided to make a big batch of deluxe macaroni and cheese.

I didn't want to use up my water, so I threw the macaroni in a pot with the last of the milk. I added in all the butter we had, too. I put the pot over the fire and stirred in the chunks of venison, the cheese from the fridge, and the powdered cheese from the box.

It was dry, with the yellow cream bubbling and mixing with the red barbeque sauce in the bottom. The powdered cheese congealed into densely packed orange clumps of flavor. It didn't look terribly appetizing, but the aroma of the cooking meat made my mouth water. It was a small pleasure, but after three days of emergency meal packs and canned fruit, a cheesy meaty stew was a luxury.

BEEEP! BEEEP! BEEEP! BEEEP! BEEEP!

The smoldering pot set off the battery operated fire alarm. I sprung to my feet and looked for the source of the clamor. It was a white plastic disc with a blinking red light stuck to the ceiling in the kitchen. I should have known better. These new fire alarms detected carbon monoxide, not just smoke.

I grabbed a dining room chair and placed it under the blaring smoke detector. I had just yanked it off the ceiling and pried the nine-volt battery out when suddenly...

BEEEP! BEEEP! BEEEP! BEEEP! BEEEP!

It was the smoke alarm in the hallway. I dragged the chair around the whole apartment, pulling down all the smoke detectors and removing all the batteries. Once I'd finished, I was not greeted by silence, but by the gut wrenching roar of the lamebrain in the hall.

The alarms had really riled up the lamebrain. It was pounding and clawing wildly at the door, but what really freaked me out was that after three days without food or water it didn't sound any weaker from hunger. It was more determined than ever. The door rattled and began to splinter under the constant pounding. It seemed like the creature might even break it down.

I leapt into action, pulling the doors off all the kitchen cabinets and nailing them to the front door. The hammering enraged the lamebrain even more, but it had to be done. I was frantic, desperately trying to cover the door jamb, while also reinforcing anywhere it looked like it might actually pound through.

As soon as I finished, I was confronted by the smell of smoke. I turned to see black smoke billowing out of the Dutch oven. The cream had cooked off and the cheese was burned to the bottom. The macaroni was reduced to dry hard crisps. Nothing edible was left.

I snapped, flinging myself at the door, determined to dispatch the lamebrain with my bare hands if I had to. I yanked at the cabinet doors I'd just finished nailing up, but couldn't pry them off, so I pounded back as it pounded, screaming wild unintelligible obscenities until I either blacked out, or passed out from exhaustion. I don't know which.

When I woke up, the fire had burned out. At least I knew my makeshift fireplace wouldn't burn the place down, but that didn't mean it was safe. If the fire gave off enough carbon monoxide to set off the alarms, I might have been poisoning myself without even knowing it. I'd have to do any cooking on the balcony, which was dangerously visible to the lamebrains below. I had mushrooms, green peppers, zucchini, and onions that would go bad. I didn't really like veggies, but I choked them down raw.

A day later, the creature went back to just waiting.

I completely underestimated what idle time would be like without power. I was going stir crazy. I alphabetized the pantry, then I organized it into food groups, and finally by expiration date. That was the most rational. I moved the furniture about ten times. At first I made barricades, then I devised elaborate traps, but eventually I was building forts, just for fun. I sorted all my clothes by color, and then all Dad's clothes by color, and then all our books and DVDs by color. I was just keeping my mind occupied. They say extreme isolation can drive you nuts.

After three weeks, the lamebrain in the hall hadn't changed at all, and I hadn't seen anything but lamebrains outside. Some days, there were dozens of them right outside my balcony. Other days, there were none. Occasionally, a car alarm went off somewhere in the compound and I watched droves of them come out of their hiding places and follow the sound. In the front of the herd were those that could actually manage an awkward sort of run. They were also the most vocal. In the middle, the majority of them shambled by in a stunted jittery walk. They mostly moaned, but didn't shout or snarl much. And behind them were the broken ones, limping, crawling or even dragging their crippled bodies across the pavement.

Then they were gone, or at least they were out of sight. But they left a trail of deep red splats and streaks that wouldn't let me forget they'd been there. Watching them come and go was like watching an ocean tide. I couldn't look anymore.

One day I woke up to the sound of screaming outside. Human screaming. It sounded like another unfortunate victim failed to escape the growing herd at the front gate. I looked out my window. It was a girl not much older than me, a redhead in a green hoodie. She was running through the parking lot, followed by a lamebrain in a Postman's uniform. It was faster than the others, and less clumsy. At first I didn't even think it was one of them, but once I saw its gray face I had no doubt. Not only that, the blood on its face and chest told me this one had fed. The girl ran out of sight, and the Postman gave chase.

I ran to the balcony, but the girl was nowhere to be seen. I had been avoiding checking on Dad, but I looked down. Its broken body looked so pathetic just lying there unable to move. But that brain-dead heap of shattered bones was my dad, and in some sense it was still alive. Maybe doctors could fix him up. If I found a cure, maybe I could bring him back, and we could go back to the way things were before.

Seven: Break On Through

I moved into the master bedroom because it was warmer. I cleared it out, and moved everything with any survival utility into the closet. Everything else I either piled against the front door as a barricade, or piled in the living room to be used as firewood. Most of my supplies were canned food and dry food. I wasn't cooking over a fire because it wasn't safe, but when it got cold enough I wouldn't have any choice.

When I pulled the bed off the wall and set it back on the ground I noticed a triangle-shaped hole in the wall where the corner of bed punched through. It gave me an idea. I had a multi-tool from my PorcScounts survival training, and it had a screwdriver. I poked around the hole, sprinkling chalky residue onto the bed. The drywall was brittle, and it was easy to widen the hole.

I ran to the kitchen and grabbed the longest knife I had. It was a serrated bread knife, which I used it to saw a hole in the drywall big enough for my head. I was careful to be as quiet as possible, pushing and pulling the knife in long slow strokes. The wall was filled with puffy, pink insulation. It was dry and itchy. On the other side was the drywall of the apartment next door.

I took out my screwdriver tool again, but then I paused. The fourth rule of PorcScouts is, *Be a good neighbor.* I was about to break into someone's home. This was their property. I wondered if that made me a bad neighbor. There was no way to know if they were even alive in there, but then there was no way to know if they were dead, either. I tried to imagine if the situation were reversed. If my neighbor had the idea before me, and they decided to break into my home, how would I feel? After everything that had happened, I'd be overjoyed just to know that someone else was alive.

I spun the screwdriver like a drill, and shoved it through as quietly as possible, making a hole barely big enough to peek in.

The room on the other side was dark. It was cluttered but it looked like the work of a slob, not a lamebrain. Best of all, it looked like no one was home. I moved the screwdriver back and forth widening the hole enough to look around. There was laundry piled in a corner, and a disheveled twin sized bed with orange sheets. Directly across from my new peephole was a bookshelf filled with comic books, and pocket change piled on a dresser. In another corner I could see that the bedroom door was wide open, and there was no telling who, or what, was lurking in the hall.

PorcScouts Rule #72, *Start every journey with a map*. This was more of a mission than a journey, but it was still a good rule. I began to sketch a map in the journal pages of my PorcScouts Survival Guide.

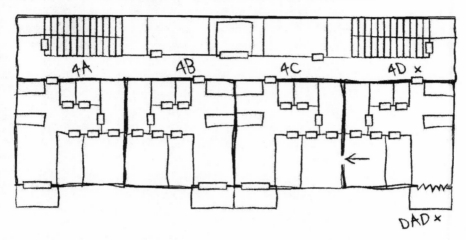

I drew my apartment, Unit 4D. The front door was on the north wall and the balcony was on the south. The kitchen and living room were on the east side, and on the west side was a hallway leading to my room, Dad's room, our shared bathroom, the hall closet and the pantry.

This was the apartment at the east end of the tower, so the exterior wall in the living room was cinder block, not drywall. I couldn't saw through that. But Dad's bedroom and the bathroom both shared a wall with Unit 4C, so either was a potential point of exit. The master bedroom in 4C was a mirror image of Dad's room, so I assumed the entire floor plan was the same but reversed. I added that to my map.

There were only four apartments on that floor. The elevator and the laundry room were in the center of the hallway, and there was a stairwell at both ends. If I could safely break through to apartment 4C, and then break on through to 4B and 4A, I could make a run for the stairs on the other side of the building, and as long as I closed the door behind me, the lamebrain in the hall couldn't follow me.

I had to be strategic about this. Each apartment along the way could be a treasure trove of supplies and gear, but there was also a good chance that there were more lamebrains inside.

33

If I was going to go through the wall, I was going to go prepared.

I dumped out my book bag, which was full of study packets and homework assignments. My report on Abraham Lincoln tumbled out. I got a D because apparently the teacher didn't agree with my interpretation of Lincoln's first inaugural address. It seemed so trivial now. I wondered if anyone would ever write about the Walking Hunger plague, or if anyone would be left to read about it.

I needed to pack everything I'd need and bring it with me. I could get cut off, or backed into another room, and not be able to get back.

I fashioned myself a utility belt out of duct tape that held my multi-tool, the bread knife, a hammer and a sack of nails. For food I packed cans from the pantry instead of dry food from the emergency kit. Cans are heavy, but they are good because they also contain water. Dry food is better for long distances. I also put a roll of duct tape on each wrist, because it's good for everything.

I widened the peephole with the screwdriver, and began cutting slowly and quietly with the bread knife. I figured that I was smaller than most lamebrains, so I tried to cut a circle just big enough for me, but too small for them. It wouldn't stop them, but it might slow them down long enough for me to make a quick retreat and close the next door.

Once the hole was cut, I needed to bust in and shut the bedroom door as fast as possible. I peered through the peephole one last time to make sure the coast was clear. I had to be fast, and I had to be completely silent. I was ready.

Eight: Stinky Romero

I pried the circle of drywall out of the hole in one swift motion so it didn't fall into the room. Then the smell hit me. It was just like the stench of the lamebrain in the hall, but aged. On top of everything else, it had a yeasty odor, like old gym socks. Something was dead inside.

I wretched a little bit. I tried to muffle it, but it slipped out. I'd broken the silence. I froze, peering into the darkness and listened.

Suddenly, a putrid smelling ball of black hair charged at me through the opening. I fell back on the bed, scrambling for the hammer, but the dark intruder didn't attack me. It hid behind me.

It was a black cat, with white patches like a tuxedo. From the look of its body language, it was being hunted. I had to get inside and get the bedroom door closed as fast as possible.

I slipped in as quiet as a ninja and moved across the room without making a sound. Behind me, the cat was peeking in, watching from the other side of the wall.

It let out a low howl, as if to warn me. I would have preferred silence.

Just as I was closing the bedroom door, it burst open, knocking me to the ground. The lamebrain of Unit 4C was standing over me. My throat constricted and my heart stopped. I was doomed.

I rushed for the nearest exit, which was not the opening in the wall, but the open bathroom door. I was almost in when the lamebrain's clammy fingers grabbed me by the book bag. I yanked hard and when it tugged back I slammed the bathroom door, so all its strength and mine crushed its arm in the door jamb.

Bones snapped with an audible pop, and the crushed forearm muscles released their grip, but it didn't retract its arm. When a normal person's limb is smashed they usually pull it back. This lamebrain had no such reflex. Instead it pressed forward, thrashing with its broken arm and trying to force the door open.

I dropped to the ground and pressed my back against the door. I braced my legs against the base of the toilet and sink so my whole body became a door stop. What the heck was I going to do now? I couldn't close the door with its arm in the jamb. If it didn't react to pain, I couldn't get it to pull out. I thought briefly about trying to cut it off with the bread knife, but I didn't have the strength to hold the door without both of my arms, and the way the broken limb was flopping wildly, I probably couldn't cut into it, anyway.

The lamebrain was irate at this point. It couldn't see me, but it had a desperate disappointment about losing a meal it just had in its grasp. Luckily, the intruding arm was so damaged it didn't have much grip left in it. It just flailed around, searching for me.

My heart was pounding so loud I couldn't hear myself think, but if I didn't act fast I was going to get tired and it wasn't. That would be the end of me.

The image of a Chinese finger trap popped into my head. It's a tube shaped toy. You put a finger in each end, but when you try to pull them out, the trap tightens. The harder you pull, the tighter it gets. The trick is you have to push in, even though it's counter intuitive. Once it's loose enough, you can pull your fingers out.

If I couldn't push the lamebrain out... I had to pull it in.

I grabbed the arm, and the next time it slammed its body against the door I pulled hard, letting the door swing open and using the creature's own momentum to launch it into the bathtub. It slipped and crashed into the tub, tangled in the shower curtain. It wasn't going to stay down for good, but the stunt bought me enough time to get out.

I made it into the hall and slammed the door behind me, but the bathroom had two entrances, one in the hall and one in the bedroom. I ran around and pulled the door in the bedroom closed, too. Then it was trapped in the bathroom. It could pound all it wanted. It was neutralized.

I closed myself in the bedroom, just in case there was another creature in the apartment, and looked for something to board up the bathroom door. I flipped the mattress, and underneath were sixteen wooden support slats that were part of the bed frame. *Perfect!*

I nailed up two of the slats across the bathroom door, but then I noticed the lamebrain was barely pounding at all. With the broken arm it didn't have enough strength to do much damage, anyway, so I set the other fourteen slats aside for firewood.

The cat came rubbing up against my leg, and he stank like the dead. He must have been trapped in there with the lamebrain the whole time. It was comforting to know that something could survive.

"Hey cat." I picked him up and scratched his belly. He was well fed, but starved for attention. "What's your name?" He had a collar, but no tags. I looked around the room for a clue and spotted an envelope on the nightstand addressed to "Mr. Romero." That must be the lamebrain's name.

"How about if I call you Stinky Romero?"

He purred his approval.

Nine: "Alive in 4D"

Stinky wouldn't leave my side after that, at least not voluntarily. He was constantly underfoot, and the moment I sat down to do anything he jumped in my lap. It would have been aggravating if not for his purring, which made him tolerable, even welcome.

He investigated my apartment as eagerly, and carefully, as I investigated his. There weren't any more lamebrains in Mr. Romero's place. He must have lived alone with Stinky. Mr. Romero was an older guy who moved in about a month before the outbreak. He kept to himself, and almost never left his apartment. I'd never actually met him.

I checked on the lamebrain in the hall, then I circled around to Mr. Romero's front door, opened it, and peeked out. The putrid smell wafted in. It was the first view of the hallway I'd had since the outbreak. It was much darker than I expected. There was only one small ventilation window on the east wall, so it would be brightest first thing in the morning.

The lamebrain looked the same as the first day I saw it, knees locked back, chest pressed against the door. The other end of the hall was dark, but I could estimate the distance from the dim beams of light shining through each peephole. I didn't want to risk making a run for it yet. I pulled back in before the creature caught my scent.

Mr. Romero was still stuck in the bathroom. I pressed my ear against the door to listen. I could tell by the sound that it wasn't staying still like the lamebrain in the hall. It could probably hear me moving around in the adjacent rooms. But it also stopped pounding faster than the other one. It was almost like it knew it was injured and gave up trying. Stranger still, it made other sounds, like it was fumbling with objects.

It was weak and trapped, so I didn't worry much about it.

There was a forty pound bag of dry cat food that Stinky had clawed open and spilled all over the living room floor. There was about half left.

38

I was amazed that he managed to get enough to eat while trapped in here with Mr. Romero, especially since it made such a loud crunching sound when he ate. The food was in the middle of the floor, not dragged under the coffee table, behind the couch, or into some other hiding place. Strange.

As I was scooping the cat food back into the bag, I heard a distinct cooing and fluttering coming from the balcony. I looked through the curtain. Mr. Romero had been growing tomatoes, lots of them. There were multiple tiers of potted tomato plants, all connected by a network of tubing such that they could be watered all at once from a funnel. Most of them were dried up, and what was left had been laid siege by a flock of pigeons. They'd built half a dozen nests around the balcony.

I threw open the curtains and the balcony door, both to air out the stink, and to let the pigeons in. It also brightened up the place. I could eat a pigeon if I had to, and I figured they'd be easier to hunt if they were inside. Maybe they tasted like chicken.

I wasn't planning to be there long enough to grow food, and I didn't have the water to spare trying to revive the plants, but I took the gardening equipment, and some seeds, and put them with my other gear. They might be useful later.

Mr. Romero's kitchen was disgusting. It looked like somebody butchered an animal in there. Red sludge in pots on the stove, in the sink, on the walls. At first I thought the lamebrain had learned to cook. Then I realized it was all dried ketchup. The weirdest thing was the fridge. It was full of ketchup in numbered plastic tubs. There were easily ten gallons of it, and from the smell of it, it was going bad.

Other than that, I found mostly cans of tuna and bags of soggy, once-frozen onion rings. There were lots of spices, but everything else had gone bad.

The second bedroom was a home office, but it looked more like the laboratory of a mad scientist. There was a desk and computer like you'd expect, but there was also a top loading refrigerator filled with still more ketchup. Talk about obsession. There was a digital camera set up on a tripod, pointed at a light box, the kind they used to take professional catalog photos. There was a big white board like the ones at school, which was covered with complex notes on a heavily edited ketchup recipe. I also found a stack of preprinted ketchup labels.

39

Mr. Romero was a ketchup entrepreneur, running a small business from home. What an interesting line of work. If only I could find some use for gallons and gallons of rancid ketchup.

That night, Stinky insisted on crawling into bed with me, no matter how many times I kicked him out. I couldn't get to sleep with the nasty smell. Maybe it was a waste of water, but I had to give him a bath. I poured about a gallon of water into a big spaghetti pot I found in Mr. Romero's kitchen, and I scrubbed him with lavender dish soap. He hated it! His howling probably woke every lamebrain in the building, but it had to be done. It didn't even get all the stink off him, but it was worth it. Having him in bed with me went a long way to keep me warm. He was like a furnace with fur.

The next morning I woke up and there was blood in my sheets. I leapt up, tore the covers away, and saw a dead pigeon in the middle of the bed. Stinky was sitting on a pillow, licking his paws and looking very satisfied with himself. I'm guessing this was his way of thanking me. Kind of a gross gift, but waste not, want not.

I'd watched Dad prep partridge for dinner before, but the breast was the only meaty part worth eating. Stinky was happy to have the wings and thighs prepared for him. It was a dark meat. I put the breast into a sauce pan with a can of cream of mushroom soup, teriyaki sauce and some Cajun spices I found in Mr. Romero's cupboards. I cooked it over my Dutch oven, but this time I set it up on the balcony where it wouldn't smoke up the apartment. I hung the bloody sheets over the rail to avoid being seen. I couldn't spare the water to wash them, anyway.

The bird was edible. If it had lived in the city, where the pigeons eat garbage, it would probably have been gross, but out here in the mountains they thrive on bugs, worms and seeds like any other bird. It was good to have fresh meat.

The bloody sheets gave me an idea. PorcScouts Rule #68, *Camouflage if you want to hide. Signal if you want to be found.*

I needed a distress signal. Using the ketchup as paint, and the ruined sheets as a banner, I hung a sign off my balcony that read, "Alive in 4D."

Ten: The Pigeon Experiment

Breaking into Mr. Romero's apartment was a victory. I doubled my floor space. I found more food, I trapped another lamebrain, and I befriended a cat. But I was still living day-to-day, and water was running out, so it was no time to get comfortable.

Something kept nagging me about Stinky. Dad's email said that lamebrains eat animals, and Stinky definitely seemed like he was being hunted, but he survived for weeks locked in that apartment with Mr. Romero. How? I had to know. I picked him up off my lap and held him to my face, "How did you survive, Stinky Romero? Tell me your secrets."

He meowed.

I didn't know for sure, but it seemed from the beginning that the lamebrains relied heavily on smell. So, it seemed reasonable to think Stinky survived because he stank. The whole apartment stank. Maybe it threw them off, made it hard to tell the living from the dead. To know for sure, I needed to devise an experiment. It was time to be a scientist.

I erased Mr. Romero's ketchup recipe from the white board and wrote "Subject: Mr. Romero."

I took a clipboard from his desk, and put on a rain poncho I found, since I didn't have a lab coat. There was battery life left in Dad's zPad so I used it to record my work. I'd seen Dad do that when he was trying to work out a problem scientifically. I'm sure he had a good reason.

"This is Dr. Max Hartwell, and this is day one of lamebrain research at Romero Labs. The subject is suffering from Walking Hunger and the transformation is complete. We have observed it trying to eat human flesh."

I wrote out the elements of the scientific method on the clipboard. "Question. Research. Hypothesis. Experiment. Analysis. Conclusion."

"First to formulate a question. Do lamebrains attack people that smell dead?" I wrote the question on the clipboard.

I thought for a moment, and chewed on the end of my pen. Then I crossed out the question and rewrote it.

"Correction. Do lamebrains attack people they can't smell?"

"Researchers at the Fr33 Aid Virology Lab observed lamebrains eating animals, not just people. In addition, it has been observed by this scientist that lamebrains track people by smell."

Under "Research" I wrote down "Smell" and drew a face with a big nose smelling a skunk.

"We hypothesize that if the subject can't track prey by smell, it won't attack the animal, and therefore if people can cover their smell, they can avoid lamebrains, too."

Under "Hypothesis" I drew a picture of me and Mr. Romero smiling and holding hands.

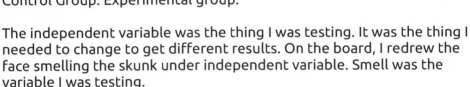

I stopped the recording. How was I going to craft this experiment? I went to the white board and wrote out the parts of an experiment.

Independent variable. Dependent variable. Control Group. Experimental group."

The independent variable was the thing I was testing. It was the thing I needed to change to get different results. On the board, I redrew the face smelling the skunk under independent variable. Smell was the variable I was testing.

The dependent variable was the outcome that changed based on changing the independent variable. I wrote, "Eating" and drew a lamebrain with a mouth full of sharp teeth on the board.

The control group was the thing I was testing without changing the smell, and the experimental group was anything I tested with an altered smell. I put some thought into this and decided to use pigeons. But first I had to confirm that lamebrains would eat pigeons, and to do that I had to catch one.

I moved all the tomato plants into Mr. Romero's living room to lure the pigeons in. Then I emptied out a laundry basket and used it to capture a pigeon. This was surprisingly easier than I thought it would be. As far as they were concerned, they were in their home, so they were pretty calm. It took a couple tries, which Stinky found utterly fascinating. On my first attempt the pigeon I tried to catch just fluttered away, which spooked all the others. If I moved slowly, and tried not to startle them, it was easy to drop the basket over one and drag it into the hall without freaking out the others.

Getting it into the bathroom was a different trick. I left the basket next to the bathroom door in the hallway, and then I started pounding on the bathroom door in the bedroom to get Mr. Romero's attention. Once it was thumping on the bedroom door I knew its back was turned to the hallway door, so I quickly scooped the pigeon in, and shut the door again.

Observing the results was difficult. All I could do was listen and record my findings.

I spoke into the zPad camera. "Once the control group was introduced, the subject stopped thumping on the bedroom door, but did not begin thumping on the hallway door. Instead there was silence, then fluttering, then growling, then munching, and then silence again. I have confirmed that the subject will attack and eat the control group."

Then I had a problem. My experimental group had to be a pigeon with its smell altered, but there was no way to make a pigeon smell like a lamebrain. I had an idea, though. I ran to my bathroom and grabbed a spray air freshener called *Free Breeze* from under the sink. Pine. They advertised that it doesn't just mask odors like other air fresheners, but it actually eliminates odors. It contains a chemical called beta-cyclodextrin which bonds with stinky molecules and prevents them from reaching odor receptors in the nose. So, if I couldn't get a pigeon to smell like a lamebrain, maybe it was enough if it didn't smell like a pigeon. It wasn't like lamebrains ate pine trees.

I captured a second pigeon, only this time I sprayed it with air freshener while it was in the basket. I distracted Mr. Romero again, and shoved the pine-scented pigeon into the bathroom. I recorded my findings.

"There was no silence this time. The subject began thumping on the hallway door instead of attacking the experimental group. After a few minutes, the subject stopped thumping, and I thought the experimental group might survive, but then the bird began to coo. The thumping immediately stopped, replaced by loud crashes. Then the fluttering and the growling, more crashing, and finally the munching."

There were still areas left on my clipboard, *analysis* and *conclusion*. I scribbled some notes and spoke into the camera, "We have confirmed that the subject is attracted to the control group by smell, because the experiment took place in the dark. The control group remained silent for the beginning of the first test, so we know that the subject's initial attraction was due to smell. So, our hypothesis is partially confirmed. However, in the second test the subject still ate the experimental group. It took longer, so we can confirm that eliminating odor offers some protection, but the subject attacked as soon as the experimental group made distinctly animal sounds."

I crossed out the drawing of me and Mr. Romero holding hands, and took off the poncho lab coat.

I put the zPad with my other gear. I wanted to keep a record of the experiment, and I would use it again if I ever devised another experiment.

The most important part of the scientific method was in the conclusion, when you admit the shortcomings of the experiment and suggest avenues of further research. The biggest problem with this experiment was that I couldn't see Mr. Romero's reactions. I had to listen. Even though I found out lamebrains are attracted to smell and sound, I pretty much already knew that.

I devised a third test. This time I went into my bathroom with the multi-tool and drilled a peephole in the wall so I could observe. There was just one problem. There were no windows in there. It was pitch black inside. I grabbed two glow sticks from the emergency kit and threw them in with Mr. Romero.

It was the first good look I'd had at Mr. Romero. In the green light of that glow stick, I could see it was dressed in a bright orange Hawaiian shirt and thick reading glasses with big black rims. It seemed like an odd thing for a walking corpse to wear, but I guess the undead aren't picky.

I set up the zPad in my bathroom to record Mr. Romero through the peephole, then I threw in another pine-scented pigeon. The reaction sounded the same at first. Mr. Romero was pounding on the door and ignoring the bird. But I didn't hear any cooing before it attacked the bird. Once it was over, I ran back to the laboratory to review the recording.

Mr. Romero didn't notice the pigeon right away. In fact, it ignored it for a while, busy pounding on the door. But once it saw the pigeon it wasted no time and seized upon it. The video was gruesome to watch, and especially creepy because the green light of the glow sticks made it look like night vision, complete with making Mr. Romero's eyes glow while it was eating. But then I knew. I could use the Free Breeze to cover my smell, but if I made a human sound, or acted too human they'd attack. The problem was I only had one can of air freshener, and it felt about half empty.

The zPad battery died after that, but there was life left in the glow sticks, so I watched Mr. Romero a while longer. I wanted to take full advantage of the light before it burned out. It didn't finish eating the pigeons. It just got tired of gnawing on them. When it was done it did something completely unexpected. It didn't go back to pounding on the door, or go into a standby mode like the one in the hall. Mr. Romero spotted itself in the bathroom mirror, and after a long time of looking at itself, it grabbed the disposable razor off the counter and began clumsily scraping its cheeks.

Eleven: Caging the Coopers

I drilled a new peephole through Mr. Romero's western wall and I could tell immediately that getting into Unit 4B was going to be a much greater challenge, because there were already two lamebrains right on the other side of the wall. Mr. Romero's place only shared one wall with Unit 4B. The living room and kitchen were only separated by a countertop, so really it was just one big room.

I was stumped.

I discovered that, if I knocked on the wall I could get the lamebrains to move to where I wanted them in the room. That was good, but not immediately useful.

I went back to my living room in 4D. It was the same layout as 4B, so it was a good place to practice. I could draw them into the kitchen, and then go in through the living room. Maybe the counter would be enough of an obstruction to buy me some time, but time for what? Alternatively, I could draw them into the back of the living room and come in through the kitchen. If I went in low I could probably stay behind the counter where they couldn't see me. But that wouldn't solve the problem, either.

Once I got in, it would just be me in a room with two lamebrains. What would my next move be? From the end of the counter it was a straight shot into the back bedrooms, but even if I rushed passed them I'd just end up cut off from all my supplies. I might even end up stuck in a room with another lamebrain. Where there was a couple, there might be children. That was no solution.

The way I saw it, I had three options. Option one, forget Unit 4B and make a break for the stairs from Mr. Romero's door, which was possible. Option two, bust into the kitchen and get the lamebrains to chase me into the hall. Then run back into Mr. Romero's place before the lamebrain in the hall got me. Then close all the doors and lock them all out in the hall. It was risky, but also possible. The downside was that all three would be in the hall later when I tried to escape. Option three, get the lamebrains onto the balcony and knock them over the edge somehow. The problem with all of those plans was that there were too many things that could go wrong.

Finally, I had an idea I was certain would work. All I needed was a smoke detector.

This was going to be my most dangerous mission so far. So, in addition to my book bag, and my utility belt, I reinforced Mr. Romero's poncho with duct tape. They may be undead, but they had human teeth. I bit into the roll of duct tape as hard as I could and only broke one layer. So I covered the poncho in two layers.

Knock, knock, knock.

I knocked on the walls in Mr. Romero's living room until I heard both lamebrains knocking back in the room next door. Once they were distracted I got to work cutting a hole in the kitchen wall. I had to be slower and quieter than before, and I periodically knocked the wall in the living room again, to keep them interested.

Once the hole was cut, I spritzed myself with air freshener and crawled in, creeping along the tile floor behind the counter. I peeked over the counter. The man had its ear pressed up against the wall like it was listening, and the woman was distracted by the fluttering of pigeons on the balcony. The duct tape was stiff and made a crinkling noise when I moved, but neither of them sensed my presence in the slightest.

Then I realized Stinky had followed me in. I shooed him away with my hand, but he didn't get it. I stuck out my tongue, crossed my eyes, and reached my arms forward, the internationally recognized signal for the walking dead. He understood. I could see the fear in his eyes, but he just meowed.

My heart sank.

I peeked again. The husband was looking around. It heard Stinky, but it didn't know where the sound came from. It started slowly dragging its feet in our direction, and the soft, uncertain grunts it made got the wife's attention.

I had to move fast.

I set off the smoke detector using a match. It was a deafening siren, louder than I expected. That got their attention, and sent Stinky running back through the wall. Then, crouched at the end of the counter, and without stepping into view, I aimed for the open master bedroom. It was a tough shot, but I had practiced it in my apartment to be sure I

47

could do it. I'd just never done it under pressure. I lobbed it underhand. It rolled diagonally down the hallway, through the open door, and ricocheted somewhere inside. *Yes!*

I watched the couple shuffle down the hall, chasing the sound. As soon as they went in, I bound after them and slammed the bedroom door behind them. Success!

The bedroom doors locked from the inside, but luckily lamebrains are too stupid to turn a doorknob. I gave a sigh of relief.

Suddenly, I heard Stinky hissing at the end of the hall. I looked up and saw a girl, about my age, with blonde hair and a yellow sweater peeking out of the other bedroom. Her back was to me and she was focused on Stinky. His ears were straight back, his back was arched, his tiny fangs were out, and his eyes were locked on her. He mustered his most ferocious roar, but it was more of a shriek.

"Karen!" I exclaimed.

It was Karen Cooper. I knew her from school. The lamebrains caged in the master bedroom must have been her parents, Harry and Helen. She was nice. Really good at art.

As soon as Karen heard me she turned her attention from Stinky to me. That's when I saw the bite taken out of her cheek and the dried red stain down the front of her yellow sweater. There was no recognition or familiarity in its eyes, although it did look glad to see me.

It reached out and came running at me, screaming. I fumbled for my utility belt and managed to grab the hammer. Karen barreled into me, knocking both of us to the ground. The impact knocked the hammer out of my hand. The lamebrain came down on top of me, trying to grab enough flesh to bite. The duct tape was slick and hard to grab, but it was strong, and merciless. I seized it by the wrists, twisting back and forth, bashing its body into the walls, but with no effect. It was still pressing down on me, its drool landing on my face. It was overpowering me.

Stinky howled and pounced on its back, raking his claws in its scalp. He didn't really hurt it, but he distracted it just long enough for me to pull the sleeves of its sweater over its hands so it couldn't claw at me. I flipped it on its belly and tied the sleeves behind its back like a straitjacket. Then I quickly wrapped its mouth and eyes in duct tape.

It was restrained, blindfolded, and gagged. It convulsed wildly, but was unable to escape. I shot Stinky a look of gratitude before I grabbed Karen by the ankles and dragged it into the bathroom. I could hear the Coopers pounding on the other door, and what sounded like an army of lamebrains pounding on the walls of the apartment next door. I should have guessed that the fire alarm would attract any lamebrains in the next unit. I locked Karen inside.

This was the end of my tunnel through the walls. With the master bedroom and the bathroom occupied, and all the pounding coming from next door, there was no way to break into Unit 4A.

I was going to have to make a run from Karen's door to the stairs. I had half the distance the lamebrain in the hall had. I could outrun it. I decided to go at dawn when the light was the brightest. So, I had all night to search Karen's place for gear, and prepare for my escape. With all the Coopers caged in their rooms, the rest of the apartment was mine to scavenge.

Twelve: Karen's Room

From the look of it, the Coopers lived a lot longer than Mr. Romero. They'd already eaten all their food, but after that they must have just holed up rather than risked going out to look for supplies. Whichever one of them died first must have changed and tried to eat the others. If only I'd gotten there sooner, I may have been able to help.

There was pretty much nothing useful in their apartment. There was plenty of furniture that I could use as firewood, and blankets, but their home was full of ornamental knick knacks, and not much else.

The door to Karen's room had a big purple pirate flag on it that read "KEEP OUT" in bone letters. I had never been in a girl's room before, at least not a girl my age. It wasn't what I expected. I thought girls liked pink lace and unicorns. Her dresser was checkered like a chessboard, except all the black squares were painted random other colors, probably by her. Her desk was painted to look like vines were growing up the legs and blooming into a bed of orange flowers on the desktop. Her computer monitor was painted to match.

Above her bed was a poster of actor Chandler Riggs, in his oversized sheriff's hat and wolf paw baseball shirt. I never got what girls liked about him. The poster was even signed. It read "To Karen, Stay Human! Chandler Riggs." So much for that.

One wall was decorated with a novelty New Hampshire license plate collection, and lined with blue lights. On the opposite wall there were different kinds of hats, including an orange beret with a shiny B17 Bomber badge, and a green Robin Hood archer hat with a long pheasant feather.

Under the hats was an acoustic guitar, and a severed parking meter leaning against the wall. I assumed that it wasn't acquired legally.

Below her window was some kind of habitat. It was a small kiddie pool filled with sand. In it there was a plastic palm tree, a cardboard castle, a miniature beach chair, and an umbrella. It looked like something may have lived there, maybe a lizard. Whatever it was, it was gone now. Maybe she ate it.

Her bed was covered with what looked like a family quilt, and on one side it was folded over showing a blood soaked blue pillow underneath. That must have been where she changed.

In the nightstand next to her bed I found a hand-bound book, covered in denim cut from a pair of jeans. A leather cord came out of the pocket on the back and fastened to the brass button on the front to keep it shut. Painted in green on the cover and along the spine were the words, "Grass Stains: The Diary of Karen Cooper."

I sat on her bed, beside her pillow, holding her book in my hand. The title triggered a flash of memory.

***

On my first day at Thornton Middle School, I learned what grass tastes like. I might not have objected in the proper clinical setting, but having the school resource officer's equally dim-witted son, Scott shove my face in the dirt was not exactly laboratory conditions.

"Get up Hartwell! Let's see what you got." Scott pulled me up by my book bag and threw me up against a fence behind the school, while his toadies stood behind him and laughed.

I straightened my clothes, covered in grass stains and mud. "I'm not going to fight you, Scott."

"Well that's too bad, because I'm definitely going to fight you," said Scott as he removed his book bag and jacket. "Let's go. You and me. You're new here, so I'll even give you the first swing." Scott held his arms open, inviting an attack.

"You and me? Then why is your backup taking off their stuff too?" I pointed at the toadies, and Scott turned. All of Scott's friends were also removing their book bags and jackets.

"Don't get smart with me, Hartwell. Do you think I'm stupid?"

"I'm not going to lie to you, Scott..."

There was a long pause as everyone waited for me to finish the sentence. The toadies began to laugh as they realized I wasn't going to, and what that meant. As the implications trickled over Scott's brainpan, rage exploded on his face.

Scott made a fist and reached way back when suddenly a soccer ball bashed him square in the face.

"Ball!" A few yards away Karen was dribbling a second soccer ball.

Blood poured out of Scott's nose as he stumbled back, disoriented.

"Awe! What's wrong Scott? Did a little girl bruise your ugly face?"

Scott thrust his index finger out at Karen. "Stay out of this, Cooper! Don't think I won't come after you just because you're a..." The second ball struck him in the guts, knocking him flat on his back in the mud.

The bell rang as Scott's toadies collapsed in hysterical laughter.

Karen grabbed and yanked me, running back to class. "You sure know how to make friends, New Kid. What'd you do to piss off a lamebrain like Scott anyway?"

"I refused to be his lab partner for the fetal pig heart dissection lab."

Karen looked me over. "You some kind of brain?"

"You might say that."

"You're new here, right? Where are you from?"

"Oh, I'm not new in town, just new at school. I'm an unschool kid, and I told my Dad I wanted to know what public school was like, so he enrolled me."

"What the heck is an unschool?" she asked.

"Unschooling is when you don't go to government school and instead you learn by experiencing life directly. So, basically I direct my own education."

"Like homeschooling?"

"Sort of, I guess. But it's not always at home. When Dad goes to work sometimes I go with him and learn about what he does, and sometimes I stay home and do whatever interests me. I don't really need that much help learning anymore."

"Are you telling me you were free to do whatever you wanted?"

I nodded. "Pretty much. Sometimes we met up with other unschool families."

"You could play games, or travel, or anything and it counted as school? Why'd you opt in to this dump?"

We arrived back in class. I tried to take my old seat but Karen grabbed me by the collar and dragged me to an empty seat near her. "Not so fast, New Kid. You owe me for sticking my neck out for you. Looks like you're my new lab partner."

"I suppose you want me to do all the work for you, too?"

"Of course." Karen smiled. "I don't want to cut up some pig heart. Science is gross."

"Science is gross!? Science is everything. Science is medicine, technology, nutrition. Science is life!"

"Life?" Karen scoffed. "What do you know about life? Science is numbers and laws. Everything measured. Everything static. There's nothing alive about science. Art is life."

I lost my cool. "Art is dumb!"

Then Scott walked into class, his nose clogged with a bloody paper towel. Schwartz, one of his buddies began to laugh, but got a quick punch in the shoulder. The teacher scolded him for being late and told him to take his seat, which he did, but not before shooting me and Karen a vengeful stare.

***

I didn't mean it when I said art was dumb. I was just mad that she said science was gross. I never told her that, but I always wondered if she knew. Wondered what she really thought of me after that.

Of course, the answers might have been right there in her diary, but I couldn't bring myself to open it. Even after everything that had happened, her diary was still her private thoughts. There was no survival reason to violate her privacy. So, I put it back in the nightstand where I found it, but before I closed the drawer something caught my eye.

A silver pen. A heavy one. When I clicked the button a laser beam shot out. The pen cast a neon red bead on the carpet, which Stinky immediately pounced on.

I laughed as Stinky repeatedly tried and failed to capture the red dot. Leaping across the floor. Spinning in circles. Swiping at walls and furniture. I played with him until nightfall.

Thirteen: The Postman

The plan was pretty simple. Get outside, get Dad's car keys, get the survival gear bag out of the trunk, and get back to the apartment. After that I had to load up my gear, and get to the lake cabin. But even though it seemed simple in my head, it felt impossible. I hadn't seen the herd in over a week, but I knew they were out there, somewhere. It seemed insane to go outside when I was more or less secure. There was some primitive instinct in the back of my brain that just did not want to risk whatever dangers I faced outside. But rationally I had to go eventually. It was just a matter of time.

I had to prepare for anything, but I also had to pack as light as possible for this mission, and I had to be fast. I made a helmet out of one of Mr. Romero's spaghetti strainers. I filled my cargo pants pockets with small gear, like the water purification tablets, and the tube of matches. I used the duct tape to make modifications to my utility belt. I created custom holsters for the multi-tool, the hammer and the nails on my left, the Free Breeze and the bread knife on my right, and three sound bombs in the back.

A sound bomb was my own invention to distract the lamebrains. I collected all the smoke detectors from the apartments and taped a match to the back of each. That way I could strike the match and set off the alarm in one motion, and then run away as fast as possible.

My book bag was small and couldn't carry much. I took a few meal packs, a few water bottles, and six more sound bombs. I made sure to wear the book bag under the poncho so they couldn't grab it. With the hood up, the poncho covered me almost completely. It was slippery and hard to bite through. The perfect armor. But there was one thing that had to be on the outside of the poncho.

I strapped a gallon jug of Mr. Romero's ketchup to my back, upside down like a jet pack. If I had to run I could dump the red sludge and hopefully slip up whatever was chasing me.

Dawn was approaching and I was just about prepped and ready to go. I spent the remainder of the night sharpening the serrated bread knife until it could easily cut deep slashes in the sofa's leather upholstery with minimal slicing. Better safe than sorry.

When it was time to go, I opened a can of tuna for Stinky. It was the only thing that kept him off my heels long enough to slip out. I didn't want him following me this time. If he finished it before I got back there was plenty of dry food left out for him.

I grabbed Mr. Romero's gardening gloves, and an extra gallon of ketchup for the hallway. Then I peeked out Karen's door.

Lighting conditions were ideal, with the dawn sun shining right through the ventilation window on the eastern wall. The lamebrain in the hall was still pressed against my door in the same posture, and at the opposite end of the hall, the entrance to the stairwell was barely visible in the dark. I had about half the distance to the exit as the lamebrain. I was carrying a lot of gear, but I was confident the gallon of ketchup would slip him up and buy me more than enough time.

I spread the extra ketchup jug all over the floor, covering as much area as I could. I was almost done when the commotion got the lamebrain's attention, so I dropped the jug and made a break for the exit. I heard it roar as it came after me but I didn't look back. I was in a full sprint.

I reached the exit and pulled the door open. It was pitch black inside. No windows. No lights. I'd forgotten about that.

I heard the slip and crash of the lamebrain hitting the floor. I snapped my last glow stick and peered back down the hall. Its eyes caught the light and reflected right back at me. It tried to stand and fell again. The best it could do was crawl through the ketchup, reaching out and dragging itself through the slime.

Splat. Splat. Drag. Splat. Splat. Drag.

I smirked.

Suddenly, gray fingers came out of the stairwell and grabbed my arm. *Idiot!* I should have known there could be lamebrains in the stairwell.

I turned, the green glow lighting up the lamebrains face, making its orange eyes glow.

It was the Postman.

I froze, my mind cluttered with questions. *How did it get in the building? How did it get in the stairwell?*

It hissed as it chomped down on my arm, the pain shooting through my whole body.

I screamed and yanked my arm away, its fingers slipping on the duct tape. Behind it I could see six more, at least, coming up the stairs.

I bolted back down the hallway. They poured into the hall like a pack of wild animals. I kept moving, but ahead of me the other lamebrain was back on its feet and standing between me and Karen's door. I was surrounded.

I took the only available door. I ducked into the laundry room next to the elevator. The door snapped shut, but there was no deadbolt.

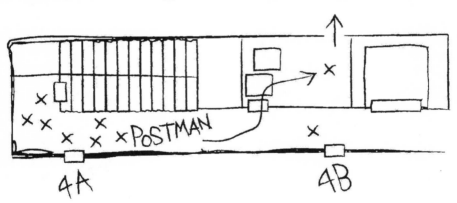

The first lamebrain smacked against the door and I knew the others were not far behind. It was a tiny room with no other doors, not even a broom closet. I pushed the washer in front of the door an instant before the avalanche of bodies slammed against it. I pushed the dryer right behind the washer when the door began to splinter. It was not going to hold.

There was a large panel on the wall. I pried it open with the back of the hammer, but it was just an electrical breaker box. No room to hide. I thought maybe if I was heavy with the air freshener I could hide in the dryer and they wouldn't find me. I had no idea what to do after that, but I was desperate.

Then I heard a sound so chilling it terrified me more than all the hissing and grunting and growling of all the lamebrains combined. I heard the distinct sound of the door knob being turned, and opened.

The door popped open, but only an inch as it hit the washer. Dozens of mangled fingers filled the gap, reaching for anything they could feed on. I watched in horror as it grew inch by inch. Then the Postman's face pressed into the opening, its hand still on the knob.

They were going to get in and there was no stopping them.

On the back wall I spotted another large panel. This one had a steel handle labeled "rubbish." I pulled it open revealing a dark chute down to the dumpsters on the first floor. The stench of stale garbage hit me in the face like salvation. I pulled it all the way open, climbed in, and just as the door was forced open and the Postman's gang poured in, I slid down, the panel springing closed behind me.

It wasn't a smooth slope. It was a four story drop straight down a stainless steel tube. I pushed my arms and legs against the sides to slow down as much as possible, and luckily the dumpster was filled with rancid trash that broke my fall.

Another advantage of the poncho was that it was waterproof.

I climbed out. I was in a small dark room on the ground floor with one dumpster. There was a thin beam of light flooding in between the double doors that lead to the parking lot outside.

I grabbed my arm, which was still aching from the bite. I examined the sleeve. Both layers of duct tape were pierced, but the poncho itself was intact. I immediately patched over the tear with another strip of duct tape. Then I pushed up my sleeve to examine the spot where it bit me. There was a deep purple bruise forming, but it hadn't broken the skin. That was close!

I checked to make sure I still had all my gear, and all my tools. I peered back up the chute. I didn't hear anything. They weren't following me. All the same, there was a hatch to close the bottom. No sense in leaving that open.

I was worried about Stinky, but he would be okay. I had no idea how I would get back up, but I'd deal with that later. My first priority was Dad's keys.

What worried me most of all was that the Postman knew how to open doors. That was new. Was it different from other lamebrains, or were they learning?

Fourteen: Goodbye Dad

It was time to sketch a new map in the journal pages of my PorcScouts Survival Guide. I had to construct the map of the compound from memory, but I did the best I could.

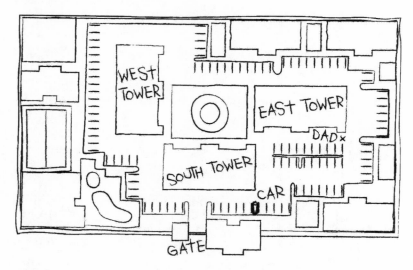

I was in the dumpster room on the north side of the east tower. Dad was on the south side, beneath our balcony. There were two other towers like ours surrounding a courtyard in the center of Lochshire Estates. One west, and one south. Our tower was east of the courtyard. The whole tower complex was surrounded by parking, which was surrounded by smaller buildings, which were surrounded by the outer wall.

Beyond the south tower, in the center of the compound's southern wall, was the entry gate, which was the only way past the compound's twelve-foot concrete wall. On one side of the gate was Sam's booth, and on the other was the maintenance facility where the staff kept cleaning supplies and repair equipment.

There were three two-story buildings along the wall, one east of the maintenance facility, and two along the northern wall near my building. On the western side of the compound there was a smaller one-story building where the nicest apartments were. It was a duplex townhome. And west of Sam's booth was the swimming pool, the leasing office, the rec center, and the tennis courts.

It was a crude map, but it was the best I had, and all that I needed to make a plan.

The double doors to the dumpster room were closed with a deadbolt I could turn from the inside, but the handles on the outside were wrapped with a chain and a padlock. I pushed the doors open about a foot before the chain pulled tight. I could just reach my arm out, and the jingling chain made more noise than I would have liked.

The lock and chain were secure, but as I felt around I found each handle was attached with six screws. The multi-tool was just the thing to take them off. I had to be careful not to accidentally drop the multi-tool outside the door, so I tied it to my wrist with the paracord.

"Righty tighty. Lefty loosey," I said to myself as I took off both handles slowly and carefully, and pulled the chain inside so the rattling wouldn't draw attention.

I peered out the crack between the doors. No lamebrains as far as I could see. *Phew!*

It was almost the same distance around the tower either way, but the last time I saw the herd it went west, so I went east.

The compound was more or less deserted. There was the occasional cadaver that was too ravaged to come back. There was a small electric car that looked like it had been torn open like a tin can, the remains of a family inside.

I moved carefully, ducking behind bushes and cars to avoid detection. A lamebrain in the back seat of a half-loaded station wagon startled me, smacking its face and palms against the car window, smearing it with blood. It was missing its two middle fingers on its left hand, and its left ear had been replaced by a grotesque bloody flap where its whole head had been gnawed on.

I recognized it. It was the boy I saw get attacked by his mom the first week. The boy slammed against the window energetically when it saw me, but it didn't try to open the car door.

"If you want to catch me so bad why don't you try the other door?" I said to it. It didn't even notice that the door on the other side of the car was left wide open. It was belted in, so it probably couldn't get out anyway.

"What's your name?" I asked.

It pressed its teeth and tongue against the glass.

"My name is Max."

I sat and watched it for a while. It was the first time I'd been that close to one, and had the time and opportunity to get a good look at it. I continued, "Where did your mom and dad go? Did they join the herd?"

It showed no sign of comprehension.

"My dad changed too, but my mom's been dead for a long time... I'm alone, just like you."

I snuck around to the other side and closed the other car door, just in case. It reached across the back seat toward me, but the seatbelt kept it strapped in place. "I have to lock you in here, for my own safety. I don't know if there's anything human left in you, but I hope so." I felt sorry for it. It could have been me under different circumstances. "When I get out of here, I'll find a cure and come back for you. Your parents, too. We can bring you back." I walked away from the car, but I wasn't sure if I believed what I'd said. What if there was no cure? What if there was no coming back?

I inched up to the southeast corner of my tower and peeked around. Dad was lying on its back like always, and its intestines were spilled out on the asphalt. There were a couple of lamebrains wandering around the parking lot, but they hadn't detected me.

I could see the keys attached to Dad's belt loop with a carabiner. Stealth was the best strategy.

I spritzed myself with the air freshener so my scent didn't get its attention and I slowly skulked toward it. I kept low so the other two lamebrains wouldn't see me over the parked cars, and I circled half around so I approached from the direction of Dad's shattered legs.

I was crouched near its feet and it still hadn't detected me. The smell of its split intestines was putrid. As soon as I saw the injury up close, I knew I had to accept that Dad was gone. Even if there was a cure for the disease, his injuries were too severe. He was gone for good, and I had to survive without him.

Rather than fiddling with the carabiner I just grabbed the keys, pulled them to the end of their retractable cable and yanked. I guessed that either the cable or the belt loop would break, and I was right, but the tug got its attention. In an instant it grabbed the tail of my poncho, so when I ran its body flipped over on its belly and dragged behind me.

I tugged, but it wouldn't let go, so I reached for the hammer. I pulled back and swung wide with all my strength, making contact with the side of its head. I felt the crunch as its eye socket collapsed, but it didn't let go. I swung again, and again, and again, until I lost count. Finally, disoriented, its fingers slipped.

When it released I fell back on my butt, and scooted away. I had beaten it unrecognizable, broken its jaw, crushed its left eye, knocked out most of its teeth, and nearly bashed its nose right off its face, but I was just not strong enough to destroy it. It no longer resembled the father I loved. I took some comfort in that.

Then I snapped. I pulled my knees against my chest and began to weep loudly, letting go of everything I'd held in for the last few weeks. The disfigured monster that was once my father reoriented itself and began to drag its broken body toward me with a look of sad desperation.

It hadn't even closed half the distance when I heard the groans and shuffles of the two other lamebrains headed in my direction. They must have heard my sobs, because they hadn't seen me yet.

I wiped all the tears and snot off my face and retreated as fast as I could. Once I was around the corner and out of sight, I changed course. Between the two brick buildings on the eastern wall was a small shed that housed trash bins. The smaller buildings didn't have garbage chutes. It was three brick walls, a corrugated metal roof to keep the rain off, and a wooden gate with a latch.

I slipped inside and dropped to the ground so I could see under of the gate.

The two lamebrains turned the corner, continued in the wrong direction, and went around the next corner of my tower toward the courtyard.

They made turns. They were guessing. Interesting.

Then Dad crawled into view. When it was on its back it was as immobile as an upside down turtle, but on its belly it was mobile. Being on its belly also revealed something I hadn't noticed until then.

Clipped to the back of its pants was the other handheld radio. That was a piece of equipment too valuable to pass up.

I wasn't sure if Dad was more dangerous now or less. It was alert and mobile, and that was a disadvantage. But it was also blind in one eye, and mostly blind in the other. The thought of a turtle gave me an idea.

I grabbed a plastic garbage can, dumped it out, and turned it upside down. Using the multi-tool and the bread knife, I carved myself a big eye hole. I could hide in the can, using it like a turtle shell, holding it down for protection. I unhooked the gate's latch and crawled out.

I approached Dad from the left side, its blind side, scanning the area for more lamebrains. When it heard me scuff, it turned to look, but seeing nothing living, it continued forward. I got right alongside the limp legs it was dragging until I was within arm's reach. I lifted my shell just enough to snatch the radio, and then dropped to the ground.

Dad twisted around and wrapped its arms around the garbage can. It was too weak to lift it up. I was safe. I pressed against the inside of the garbage can, only a thin layer of plastic between me and it, and I began to cry. The more I sobbed the tighter its grip became. I fell apart. Dad's arms were wrapped around me almost like a hug, one last moment of almost human contact before I said goodbye.

Fifteen: The Herd

When there were no more tears to shed I took a deep breath, threw off the trash can, and ran away. Dad's car was parked near the maintenance facility, so I headed in that direction.

I hopped over the splat where Dad had landed from the balcony and looked up. From that angle, I could see the bloody sheets I'd used as the distress signal, but that hadn't done me any good. The situation looked very different from outside. It looked pretty easy to get from one balcony to another by climbing around the outside of the tower. Unfortunately, there was no easy way to climb from the ground to the second floor balcony, and no real way to tell from here if any balcony was safe from the lamebrains inside.

I crossed the parking lot to Dad's car in front of the maintenance facility. From there, I could see the area near the front gate about fifty feet away. At least a dozen lamebrains were crowded together in front of the closed gate. They looked even more grotesque in a group, their clothing stained by the secretions of each other's wounds. It was the look on their face that stood out most. They looked determined, but vacant. Without something readily available to consume, they had a look of nonspecific longing. Individually, the gaunt expression was unremarkable, but in a group, all with the same expression, it was their most obvious feature.

Something had attracted their attention. Maybe they were trying to get out, or maybe to them it was a buffet of anyone else trying to get out. The windows were broken out of Sam's booth, and a few lamebrains were wandering between the cars parked nearby.

They hadn't seen me, so I stayed low behind Dad's car. I unlocked and opened the driver's side door as quietly as possible, but I didn't take my eyes off them. I pulled the trunk release, which made a small click. They didn't notice.

Ducking behind the rear bumper of the car, I pushed the trunk open slowly, and spotted Dad's survival gear bag inside. It was a large black canvas backpack that was loaded with useful stuff. I reached in, snatched it, and ducked behind the bumper again. After a minute I peeked through the car windows. They still hadn't noticed me.

I threw the bag over my shoulder and began to move away slowly. It was heavy. Once I was out of sight of them, I hid behind some shrubs and looked through the bag.

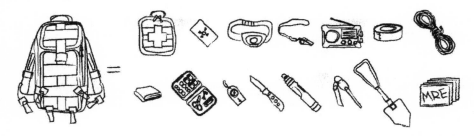

Every good bug out bag begins with a first aid kit. This one had a deluxe tactical trauma kit, able to handle the immediate needs of semi-serious injuries. For light, there was an extra bright LED lamp with a head strap. I attached it around my spaghetti strainer helmet. For communication, it had a signal mirror, a whistle and a solar and crank powered AM/FM radio. For gear, the bag had more duct tape, another fifty feet of paracord, one more emergency blanket, a sewing kit, a compass, a locking knife, a water filter, a magnesium/flint fire-starter and a compact, tri-fold shovel. The bag also contained four MRE meals.

I cinched the bag up and ran toward the front of my tower. The double doors were both wide open. I don't think anything could have freaked me out more. If they were unlocked, that would be one thing. If they were boarded up that might indicate survivors inside. But leaving the doors wide open made no sense. I guess that's how the Postman got in.

I wasn't going in there. There was no getting past the gang of lamebrains in the hall, anyway. I had another idea.

I went back to the splat under my balcony and looked for cars nearby. There was a Jeep just a few yards away. *Perfect!* A Jeep is pretty light for its size, and a manual transmission has a lot less rolling resistance than an automatic. Best of all, it was a straight shot. I could put the Jeep in neutral, push it under the balcony, and climb up.

The Jeep was locked, so I broke the window, setting off the alarm. It rang through the compound like a dinner bell. This was not going well.

I shifted the gear and got behind the Jeep. I shouldered against the back of the Jeep, rocking it forward, but then it rocked back. I pushed my back against the bumper and pushed with both my legs against the curb. It started to move, but not fast enough. The lamebrains wasted no time.

I hadn't moved the Jeep more than a few feet when I saw the first lamebrain headed my way, but it wasn't the herd coming around the corner like I expected. The lamebrains were throwing themselves off balconies to come after me.

The first one fell from the third floor and landed right beside the Jeep. Luckily, it landed on its head. *Splat!* It reminded me of the egg drop we did last year in science class. I won. It was just a matter of physics. The potential energy of the egg at the top has to be dissipated before it's converted into enough kinetic energy to break the egg. And the way you do that is to maximize the distance between where the egg is at the moment its container touches the ground, and where the egg is when it comes to full stop. In the lamebrain's case, the distance between contact and full stop was about a centimeter. Minus air friction, which is negligible.

Dad never said he was proud of me for anything, even though I always knew he was. He didn't want me to define myself according to what he thought, or what anyone else thought. He always asked me if I was proud of myself.

I snapped myself out of my physics daydream when the herd came stumbling around the corner. I tried to get the Jeep under the second story balcony before they reached me, but they covered half the distance before I did. It was time to run!

I took the gear bag and ran toward the dumpster room. I turned the first corner around my tower and ran past Dad and the garbage bin. I turned the second corner and ran toward the steel doors, but by the time I reached them the herd had already spotted me. If I locked myself in there I'd be trapped. Safe, but trapped. I had to find a way to hide, and I had to buy myself some distance.

I dropped sludge and kept running. The ketchup would at least slow them down. I ran straight past the center courtyard and into the front entrance of the west tower. They could see me the whole way, and they would follow me in, but if they didn't see me slip out the back exit maybe I could lose them inside.

The inside of the tower was deserted. No signs of life... or death. I came out the back side of the tower before they made it through the front

69

entrance. In front of me, across the parking area, was the duplex townhome. To the left was the tennis courts, and beyond that, the rec center. To the right was a garden area between the duplex and the north wall.

That's where I saw my salvation. The compound's landscaping truck was parked in front of the garden. It was a pickup with a cable winch on the front and a cage mounted to the bed to hold all the equipment. The top was open, but the sides of the cage were high enough that I'd be safe inside.

I set off all three sound bombs and threw one into the yard of the duplex, one over the fence into the tennis courts, and I rolled one down the parking lot toward the rec center. Then I ran toward the landscaping truck. The gate on the back of the cage was locked, but it was easy to climb on the hood of the truck, then on the cab, and get in from the top. I covered myself in air freshener and hid under the canvas sacks they used to haul yard clippings.

I watched as the herd came pouring into the parking lot and ran in every wrong direction. It was the middle of the day, but I was exhausted from the chase. I passed out under the canvas sacks as soon as I knew it was safe.

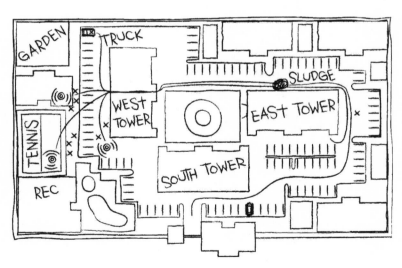

Sixteen: Daybreak

I woke up in the middle of the night. I'm not sure if it was the cold, or the sound. Probably both. Winter was approaching and a chill was in the air. Once the heat of day was gone it was difficult to stay asleep. But the moment I realized the rattling against the cage was real, and not some distant nightmare, I bolted up, wide awake. I could just barely see in the moonlight. My heart started racing.

I saw a lamebrain dressed in white shorts and a purple polo shirt. For some reason it was carrying a tennis racket.

It must have wandered over from the tennis courts near the rec center, or maybe it got infected on its way there. Either way, it was here now, and it wanted in. With its free hand it was yanking on the side of the cage, and occasionally it hit the side with the tennis racket, making a loud clang.

It wasn't using it as a club exactly. It seemed barely even aware it was carrying it. The tennis racket was just incidental, like it just never bothered dropping it.

As soon as it saw me, it let out a ravenous gurgle, subdued somewhat by having half of its neck chewed through. Hearing this, a few others wandering nearby started closing in. My pulse quickened as I felt the adrenaline course through my veins.

Was it calling them or did they just know the sounds each other made when they found food?

I took out the Free Breeze and sprayed the tennis player right in the face. It stopped gurgling and started sniffing, looking confused. I got right in its face and did my best lamebrain impression, crossing my eyes and gabbing my jaw up and down with a stupefied moan. It watched me, clearly doing something not entirely unlike thinking, and then it decided I wasn't interesting anymore. It let go of the cage, and wandered away. When the other lamebrains saw that, they lost interest, too. I breathed a sigh of relief.

They followed each other's lead. That was good to know. Maybe that's how they ended up in herds. Except these ones weren't in a herd. They were scattered apart.

I ducked back under the canvas bags. My escape could wait for daybreak.

The first sign of dawn was a gray light in the sky, followed by birds tweeting their morning song, and soon, visible light. There were at least a dozen lamebrains wandering near the landscaping truck, but none of them had detected me. Some were stumbling around the garden. Others were lurking in the parking lot. The tennis player was creeping toward the rec center. They were all searching for their next meal.

I stayed hidden under the canvas bags, and watched them while I ate an MRE for breakfast. As long as I was safe, I wanted to study their behavior. Then something strange happened.

The first direct sunlight peeked over the wall of the compound from the east and flooded the garden, including the landscaping truck. It was nice to feel a touch of warmth. When I looked behind me I nearly choked on my MRE because the lamebrains that had been wandering in different directions were now all headed toward me. My body tensed as I felt overwhelmed by a sense of doom, but they passed right by me.

I looked around and all the lamebrains that were standing in the sun were slowly moving toward the shade. It wasn't hurting them. They weren't hurrying. They just didn't like sunshine, I guess.

By the time the day was warm most of them had congregated in the shadow cast by the west tower. They weren't doing anything really. Still wandering aimlessly, just crowded together by the sunlight. That's how the herds formed!

When I saw that the dumpster room of the west tower was left open it gave me an idea. I went into the survival gear bag and pulled out the signal mirror.

Dad always preferred a low-tech solution if it meant a tool was renewable. Always chose a flint spark lighter over matches. Always picked a hand crank over extra batteries. When Dad prepped for an emergency, he prepped for sustainability. A signal mirror is the low-tech, sustainable solution to lasers and signal flares.

It was about the size of a credit card and made of a tough reflective plastic. In the center was an aiming hole. The mirrored surface focused the reflected sunlight into an intense beam, and by holding the back to my eye and viewing through the aiming hole, I can direct the beam to create a signal that's visible up to twenty miles away on a clear day.

Remembering how Stinky chased the little red bead of light from the laser pointer, I wanted to see if the lamebrains were similarly inclined. I peeked over the back of the landscaping truck with the mirror in direct sunlight and cast the beam on the back wall of the west tower to my right. The hot white bead was about the size of a silver liberty coin.

The lamebrains were herding in the center of the wall, so I placed the bead right above one the stragglers on my side of the tower, a wiry young woman in a light blue shirt that read, "Shop Smart. Shop S-Mart." I shook the beam to get its attention and sure enough, it went right for it. I lowered it to get the lamebrain to reach up, and then raised it out of reach again. After a few failed attempts it was practically climbing the wall to get it. It ground its fingertips into bloody stubs against the rough surface, leaving bright vertical red streaks on the wall.

Once I was sure I had control of S-Mart girl, I directed it over to the rest of the herd. Others that saw the bead of light went for it, too, until a bunch of them were climbing over each other to get to it. But best of all, the rest of them followed their lead. The ones in the back didn't know

73

what the ones in the front were fighting over. They just knew they wanted a piece, and once they were riled up, they started making sounds that drew out all the others from the playground and the rec center that followed the sound bombs the night before. Before long, there were at least thirty lamebrains fighting over a mirage. I found it hilarious, until I remembered these freaks were once real people.

Once all the stragglers were caught in the fray, I shined the beam into the open dumpster room. S-Mart girl went right in, and the whole herd followed in after. I saw the tennis player shamble right in. They didn't even know what they were looking for.

As soon as they were all inside, I threw off the canvas bags, grabbed a rake and a shovel, and jumped out of the truck. I moved quickly along the back of the west tower and slammed them in, crossing the rake and the shovel through the handles of the double steel doors. When I saw the chain and open padlock hanging from one handle, I wrapped it tight and locked them in. *Victory!*

I looked around to make sure I was alone. The swimming pool outside the rec center gave me another idea.

Seventeen: The Deep

I ran back to the landscaping truck. I needed some place secure while I figured things out. I got under the canvas bags and pulled out my map. Using a variety of small objects from the sewing kit and the first aid kit, I reconstructed a crude model of the compound and used the headlight to simulate the path of the sun.

At night, the lamebrains spread apart and wandered around, and in the morning the sunlight would push them east toward the shady side of buildings and walls. As the sun rose, and the shadows shrank, they would concentrate in the shadiest places. Probably the west sides of the three towers, along the eastern wall, or anywhere there was plenty of tree cover. At noon, with the sun at its highest point, and the shadows mostly gone, I guessed they would wander around again, only in herds. Then, in the evening, the setting sun would draw them west again, unless they found their way inside.

In my mind, I imagined the lamebrains flowing back and forth like the tide. Right now the tide was flowing east. Then I realized something truly chilling. The shadiest place in the whole compound was the courtyard in the center of the tower complex. Not only was it surrounded by the three towers, but it also had the most tree cover in the compound. They would congregate there. Then, when the sunlight came over the east tower and shined into the courtyard, it would drive the lamebrains right into the open doors of my building.

I ran toward the pool area, which was surrounded by a head-high wrought iron fence on three sides. It was easily strong enough to hold out a herd of lamebrains, and if necessary, hold them in. Plus, it was overgrown with ivy, creating a visual barrier.

I checked to ensure the pool area was clear of lamebrains. The west side butted up against the rec center, which included the leasing office, and the gym. Both of them were also empty, making it the perfect escape route, but before I did any planning, I stripped off all my clothes and dove into the cool water. The chlorine made the water no good for drinking, but I hadn't had a real bath since this whole thing started. I felt like the first prehistoric man who ever crawled out of the caves and jumped in a lake.

I did running cannon balls off the diving board, and swam to the bottom of the deep end until my lungs ached. I did back flips and belly flops until the air cooled, and clouds rolled in. When it began to sprinkle, I climbed out. It was good to play, to feel normal again, even briefly. But it was time to get to work.

I got dressed, double checked my survival gear bag, and stashed it in the empty rec center for safe keeping.

I gathered up a handful of stones from the planter boxes and climbed up on an equipment shed, so I could see over the fence. To my left were the tennis courts, the duplex townhome, and the west tower. To my right, I could see around the corner of the south tower to the front gate, but the lamebrains that were blocking the gate were gone. And right and front of me was a walkway between the two towers, into the courtyard. I didn't see any lamebrains inside, but if my theory was correct, that's where they went.

"Hey you, slobbering pus bags!" I chucked a rock through the towers and into the trees, hearing only the snapping of twigs and the rustle of leaves. "I know you're in there! Come and get me!"

After about a minute the first lamebrain shambled out; a pot bellied man in an orange jogging suit. It hadn't seen me yet. It just heard me. I chucked another rock and pegged it right in the nose. As its head kicked back, its right eye popped clean out of its socket and rolled into the parking area. Then I had its attention. It let out a roar I knew would call others and began running in my direction, crushing its own eye under its jogging shoes like a grape. It was fast. By the time it reached the fence, about a dozen were following it.

The wrought iron rods held against the avalanche of rancid flesh, but more were coming, so I jumped down and pulled my hammer from my utility belt. Running along the fence, I clanged the bars to lead them toward the entrance.

"All you can eat! Human buffet! First come, first serve! Follow me, you parasites!"

Through the ivy, I could see them tracking my voice, so I threw the gate open, ran to the opposite side of the pool, and climbed out on the diving board.

The rain was pouring, and the sky was dark with storm clouds. When the orange jogger came through I pelted it with another rock. The ground was so slippery it fell over, which caused a pile up at the gate.

76

"Over here, you stink buckets, you brain-dead slimes! I'm ready for you!"

The piled up corpses eventually untangled themselves and started coming at me again, some crawling, some walking clumsily and some running, but they all failed to reason their way around the pool in their way. The one-eyed-creature in the orange jumpsuit staggered right down the steps of the pool, and waded into the deep end. The others followed right behind.

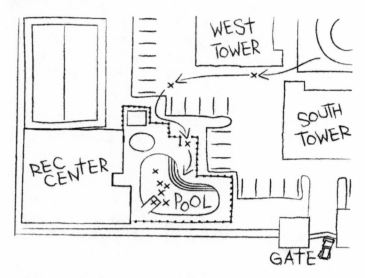

They didn't swim. They didn't float. They didn't even bubble as they went under. They just walked straight to the bottom of the pool and stopped.

PorcScouts Rule #35, *If you can't swim, stay out of the deep end.* Stupid lamebrains.

I watched them reaching up from the bottom until the water ran red and then black with their bodily fluids. More filed in, twenty at least, until the last lamebrain came through the gate and joined its comrades in the murky water. They disappeared beneath the slick black sludge.

Through flashes of lightning I could see them shifting around below the surface, grasping hands and tortured faces, and I wondered if they would drown. Did they even need oxygen?

I didn't have much time to wonder. Suddenly, one of them burst up and grasped the bottom of the diving board. The jostling of the slippery

77

board knocked me off my feet. The creature got ahold of my foot, and used it to pull itself out of the water.

It was a woman with straight black hair on one side of her head, and exposed brain on the other. Its skin was pale and wrinkled like parchment, and it was surprisingly clean from the little swim. It was climbing over a heap of bodies, all scrambling over each other to get to the top. Yanking my foot, it pulled its upper torso out of the putrid water and was inching toward me on the diving board.

Dozens of hands were pulling it back down, and me along with it. Others were reaching up and grabbing ahold of the board, hanging off the sides with their mouths chomping.

I grabbed the metal handrail to pull myself back from the edge, but the parchment faced woman had me by the leg and was gnawing on my shoe. With my free leg, I began kicking it in the face, but I couldn't dislodge its powerful jaw. The diving board began to splinter from the weight and the tip dipped all the way to the water's surface. I felt it begin to give way.

I dug the toe of my free foot under the heel of the shoe in the creature's mouth and kicked it off. My foot slipped out, which sent the parchment faced woman crashing into the water with my shoe, and slingshot me the other way as the board sprang back up.

Free, I flipped over and leapt for the edge of the pool, just as the diving board snapped beneath me and sank into the grasping mob. I scrambled across the rain soaked concrete and closed myself inside the rec center. I grabbed my survival gear bag and slipped out the rear entrance of the rec center, closing and locking the gate to the pool area on my way out.

Eighteen: Home Invasion

I headed toward the front gate. The ground was dark and sticky with lamebrain drippings. I only had one shoe, and didn't want to step in the goo, so I grabbed a new pair of shoes from the remains of a body. They weren't my style, but they came off a kid about my age, so at least they were my size.

I weaved my way through the parked vehicles to avoid detection and reached the front gate. A purple pick-up truck had slammed into the gate, knocking it off its track. Someone had tried to ram the gate from the outside, probably thinking it was safe inside. The gate was still latched closed, just bent, and if I couldn't open it, I was essentially stuck in here until I found another way out.

I reached into Sam's booth, searching for an emergency release. I found the lever and pulled it. The locking mechanism unlatched with a loud clang. I glanced around, but it didn't appear there was anything around to hear the noise. I pushed a few buttons on Sam's control panel, but it had no juice, not even from the back-up generators. I was going to have to figure another way out.

I went back to the Jeep parked under my balcony. The alarm had drained the battery and shut off, so it was safe to move it. I shouldered against the back, rolling it under the second floor balcony and climbed up.

Stinky must have heard me, because the moment I reached the second floor he poked his head between the iron bars of the railing and howled his greeting down to me.

"Hey Stinky! Did you miss me?"

He affirmed with a meek "meow," but then hissed the same warning he gave when he saw Karen. I looked out over the parking lot, but didn't see anything. The apartment on the second floor seemed quiet. He must have seen something upstairs.

It was an easy climb. At each floor I used the multi-tool to unscrew the railing from the wall, and then fastened it vertically to the floor and ceiling with the same screws to use as a ladder to the next floor.

Stinky was very happy to see me, but acted a little spastic. I'd even call it paranoid. I greeted him on the balcony and sat on the ground so he could climb in my lap. He rubbed against me affectionately as I scratched his head and neck. Once he felt properly reacquainted with me, he went to the door and meowed loudly, asking me to take action.

As soon as I stepped into the unit, I saw why. The front door and all my reinforcements had been pounded to splinters. All the doors in the unit had been bashed open and what was left was covered in bloody hand prints. A thick trail of red and black sludge snaked through the entire apartment. The Postman and its gang must have come through after I escaped down the garbage chute. Dribs and drabs of undead gore were all over everything. My water supply was completely contaminated.

Stinky was meowing incessantly the whole time. My heart was pounding as I snuck through the apartment, checking for intruders, but there were none. Mr. Romero's apartment looked the same. All the doors were bashed open and Mr. Romero was gone. Bits and pieces of feather and bone were strewn about the balcony and living room.

That's when I realized that Stinky was out of food, and the gang had devoured all the pigeons. Stinky was meowing because he was hungry. I refilled his dish with dry food, and poured him water from my bottle. He scarfed it eagerly.

Karen's parents were gone too, but I found Karen in the hallway leaning up against the elevator. Its eyes and mouth were still covered, and its arms were still tied behind its back. It must have been too disabled to follow the Postman's gang when they left. I dragged Karen back to her room and tied it to the bed. Once it was restrained, I removed everything off its face. It snapped at me and growled but it was secure. I pulled up the covers so that eventually when it starved... if it starved... it would look like she died peacefully in her bed.

I followed the trail of gore through unit 4A, which was the same as the others, with all the doors pounded into timber. Then the trail led into the stairwell.

Once he'd eaten, Stinky clung to my side, and didn't make another sound. He seemed bolder now, his tail jittering with excitement as he explored the new terrain. He followed me into the stairwell.

When I pushed the door open, I was again confronted by the darkness of the stairwell. I left my head lamp off to avoid detection and stepped down the stairs as quietly as possible. With each step, I stopped, listened, and proceeded only when I was certain it was silent.

Stinky, on the other hand, ran ahead, only occasionally pausing for me to catch up. I was only able to see him by the gleam of his eyes when he looked back at me, or the occasional sound of him scratching. I learned to rely on his eyes and ears, which were better in the dark.

I heard his signature hiss indicating danger, and saw him nudging his nose through the door on the third floor. A dim light from the hallway made him just barely visible. As I approached the door, I heard the faint slapping of dead meat against wood, but it was far away, so I continued.

I nudged the third floor door open just enough to peek around the corner. Units 3A, and 3B were already bashed open. My eyes followed the red stains along the floor to the door of unit 3C. That's when I saw Mr. Romero, the Coopers, and the rest of the lamebrain gang all pounding their way in. As soon as I saw the Postman at the head of the gang, I realized what was going on.

The Postman was enacting his residual memory, like the tennis player with its racket, or Mr. Romero shaving. But the Postman was of going door-to-door to deliver mail. In this new world, that was a search pattern, making the Postman far more dangerous than the others.

The rest of the lamebrains just followed the Postman, because that's what they do. They provided the muscle, and the Postman provided the brain, or what was left of a brain. They broke down the doors, ate whatever life they found inside, and recruited whatever was left to join the Postman's growing infectorate.

It suddenly occurred to me that I was completely exposed. No doors stood between me and the Postman's gang. They had destroyed them all, and there were at least twenty lamebrains in the group. I had to get out of there. Nowhere was safe if the Postman was systematically searching every room. It was time to leave the compound. There was just one problem. Before I could hit the road, I had to find fresh water.

Nineteen: Over The Edge

The Postman's search pattern could be a real advantage for me. Knowing this meant predicting its movement. It also meant I could be relatively certain they wouldn't come back to my apartment. Once the Postman's gang was done searching the third floor, it would be safe, as well. And then the second floor, and then the first, and then the Postman would probably leave the building, taking most of the lamebrains with it.

This also gave me a search pattern of my own. If I stayed on the Postman's heels, I could search for water in relative safety, as long as none of them caught my scent.

I started by searching unit 4A.

I didn't find water, or much of anything useful. Unit 4A was really strange. It had been the home of an elderly woman, who had presumably joined the Postman's gang. Her unit was filled with porcelain dolls, some so lifelike I almost thought they might move.

They were placed around the apartment, posed like real people. One was seated on the couch facing the TV. Another was sitting at the kitchen table with a miniature place setting. There was even one tucked into a miniature bed in the master bedroom. It was really creepy. Their glass eyes were so piercing my mind was playing tricks on me, telling me the eyes of the dolls were following me.

There was a series of photos on the wall in chronological order. A wedding photo. A tropical vacation. She seemed so vibrant and beautiful in the photographs with her husband. But in the next photo, she was alone, and in every photo after that she was more placid, and the light was gone from her eyes. In the last photo, she looked just like the porcelain dolls. There were no photos of children.

I did find a couple extra bottles of Free Breeze, which were as precious as gold. After I finished searching the unit, I added the new air freshener to the stash of gear I'd accumulated in Dad's bedroom.

Suddenly, I heard the heart halting sound of a human scream. It was female. I ran to the balcony and listened. She was right below me, in unit 3D. I slid down the impromptu ladder to the third floor balcony, but the curtains were drawn so I couldn't see inside. The sliding glass door was locked.

From the sound of it, the Postman's gang was at her door.

I slammed my hammer against the glass, cracking it but not breaking it. So, I grabbed a metal barbeque by the legs and swung hard, shattering the door to pieces.

Inside, furniture was piled up against the door, and the pounding from the other side was deafening. A panicked redheaded girl in grubby jeans and a green hoodie was pointing a revolver at me. She was about my age, maybe a year older.

"Where the heck did you come from?!" she screamed, lowering the firearm once she saw I was still human.

I stood there dumbfounded, her green eyes locked with mine. I did nothing. I said nothing.

"Don't just stand there, Kid. Help me!"

Without speaking, we pushed the couch up against the growing pile of home furnishings.

"No good. Too many. They'll get through. You've got to come with me." I grabbed her arm.

She jerked her arm and shoved me back. "Don't you touch me!"

"Sorry. But, there's no time. This won't hold them. They broke down my door, and it was way stronger than this."

Wood split and furniture shifted as the hinges and deadbolt ripped out of the door frame. The door leaned in and the first arm came through the gap up to the elbow.

She grabbed me by the arm and pushed me toward the balcony. "Okay. Let's try your plan. How do we get out of here?"

"Follow me." I climbed out onto the ladder just as the front door gave way. The pile of furniture spilled over and the first lamebrain stumbled in. It was Mr. Romero.

"Come on!" I started climbing up.

I pulled myself up to the balcony above as she swung out onto the ladder. Just as she reached the top, Mr. Romero lunged, grabbing her ankle with its one good arm before it stepped off the balcony. She screamed as she lost her grip under the extra weight. I dove to the edge, just catching her wrists with both hands.

Mr. Romero hung there, too weak to pull itself up, but heavy enough to drag us both down. Its broken arm hung lifeless by its side. The rest of the gang charged through the apartment and tumbled right over the edge. Bones snapped and metal dented as they rained down on the Jeep below.

"Don't let go!" she screamed as she kicked at the persistent creature.

"I won't drop you, but I need your help." I reached back, and my fingers found the sharpened bread knife. I held it out to her. "You've got to pry it off of you."

The first lamebrains to fall were broken and crippled, but they broke the fall of the second wave, which remained relatively uninjured down below.

She took the knife and swung at Mr. Romero's hand. She screamed as she sawed through its fingers, blood spurting as its grip released. Four gray fingertips fell to the asphalt below, followed by Mr. Romero.

The green-eyed girl sprang up onto the balcony, wrapping her arms around me. We watched in horror as the cascade of bodies dribbled to a halt.

Twenty: Gash

The ground below was covered with lamebrains, stretching their grasping hands up toward the two of us on the fourth floor. I realized the Postman was not among them. There was an eerie calm, punctuated only by the moans of the fallen when I heard its labored breathing coming from the floor below.

My eyes locked with the green-eyed girl's. She heard it too, and mouthed to me without vocalizing, "It's right under us."

I grabbed ahold of the rail and leaned out to get view of the balcony below. The Postman was standing at the edge, looking down at its mangled gang. It didn't follow the herd over the edge. Then it turned and walked away, presumably back on its search for food. It was acting independently.

I turned to the girl. "I don't think it saw us, but it's time to get out of here."

"And how do you suggest we do that?" she rebuffed.

"I have an idea. If the Postman keeps going on the same pattern, it will take the stairs to the second floor."

"Pattern?! What pattern?"

"The Postman is different. It's more intelligent than the others. I don't know why. If we take the other stairwell, we can get to the bottom before it does."

"No way. There are a hundred creepers in the lobby at least. That's how I got stuck in here."

"Creepers? Is that what you call them?"

"Yeah. What do you call them?"

"Lamebrains."

She scoffed. "Well, that's not very succinct."

"Fine, creepers then."

86

She stood up and immediately winced in pain, grabbing her ankle. Her sock was soaked through with blood. She sat back down.

"Are you okay? Let me look at that!"

"It's no big deal. I cut myself getting that creeper off my leg. I've had worse."

"Cut the tough girl act! You could get a nasty infection if we don't dress it." I sat next to her foot. "I know what I'm doing." I carefully untied her shoe and delicately peeled back the dripping sock. Blood spurted out of the open gash onto the floor.

"Wow!" She looked a little queasy when she saw the blood.

"It looks pretty deep. You might have damaged the muscle. But don't worry. I need you to put pressure here to stop the bleeding." I placed her hands on the wound and pulled the trauma kit from my survival gear bag, along with the PorcScouts Survival Guide. I flipped through the book and found the section on lacerations.

> *Treating lacerations in five easy steps: stop the bleeding, assess the damage, clean it, close it, and dress it.*

"I thought you knew what you were doing?" Her eyes grew wide.

"I do. I've just never done it." My eyes darted around the page. "Direct pressure ... gauze ... clean rag ... tourniquet ..." Then I spotted what I was looking for.

> *Memorize this saying: 'Arteries spurt. Veins ooze.' Arteries carry oxygen-rich blood from the heart to the body. Veins drain blood back to the heart.*

I turned to her. "Here's what I need you to do. I want you to release the pressure very slowly so we can see how bad the bleeding is."

She lifted her palm, but the blood was still gushing to the beat of her heart. "You've definitely nicked an artery, but don't panic. We can treat this. We need to keep pressure on it for five to ten minutes and then we'll check again."

She watched intently as I pressed a pad of sterile gauze down on her wound to hold it closed. "Where did you learn this stuff?"

"From my dad."

She caught the crack in my voice, and didn't respond. She'd lost a lot of blood and was looking a little pale. I tried to take her mind off it.

"Hey, what's your name, anyway?" I asked.

"Why?" she countered.

I was taken aback by the question. "It's just the thing you ask. My name's Max."

"Look Max. I'm not looking to make new friends. I was doing fine on my down before this. Let's just get out of here, and if we both live maybe we'll get acquainted."

"Deal. If the first floor is overrun, we'll have to find another way."

"Well I'm not climbing down there." She pointed to all the crippled creepers that were just waiting to get a bite of us. All their pus, and blood, and black goo dripped into a growing pool of glistening muck.

"What about the garbage chute?"

Wow! She was quick. "No. It's locked at the bottom." I didn't tell her I was the one who locked it. I should have known better. I checked and the bleeding had slowed. She looked relieved. "Try to wiggle your toes." She winced, but they moved just fine. "That's good. That means there's no major tendon damage. Any numbness?"

She rubbed her foot and pinched her toes. "No."

"Good. No nerve damage. How's the pain?"

"It's bad."

I dug some pain meds out of the trauma kit and handed them to her. "This isn't much, but it's the best we've got. You damaged the muscle, but it will mend. Ideally, you should keep off it, and get plenty of rest, but we don't exactly have that option. Let's clean it." I began carefully wiping the blood away from the gash with sterile swabs, careful not to push any more in, then I flushed the wound with water. "You know, this is going to need stitches."

She looked worried. "Ok. Do you know how to do that?"

I flipped the page in the PorcScouts Survival Guide.

> *If the laceration gapes open, close it with sutures. Small cuts can sometimes be closed with tape. Duct tape works well. Deeper gashes will require stitches.*

There were instructions. "I do now."

I put on a pair of latex gloves from the trauma kit, and found all the sterile swabs and gauze I needed. But the kit didn't have a needle or sutures. All it had was adhesive butterfly sutures. I had the instructions, but not the equipment.

I grabbed the smallest needle from the sewing kit, and for thread I tried an old survival trick Dad once told me about. I used the multi-tool to split the end of the paracord. The inside core was made up of small densely spun nylon fibers. Once sterilized with alcohol wipes, they made ideal sutures.

When she saw the paracord she said, "Hey, if you've got enough rope we can go to the roof and climb down the other side. It should be clear over there."

"That could work, if you feel up to it."

"No problem. I'm a lot tougher than you think."

"Let's find out. I don't have any numbing ointment, so this is going to hurt."

She nodded as she bit her lower lip.

To her credit, the only pain she showed was a little squeak the first time the needle went in. It was kind of cute. The first three stitches were a little crooked, but I quickly got the hang of it. It was just a simple square knot. There were thirteen stitches in all. "This is probably going to leave a scar," I warned.

"Awesome!" Her eyes lit up. "Every survivor should have a good scar in a world like this."

When I finished I tied off the thread and continued reading.

> Apply a cotton pad, gauze, or other sterile dressing. If possible, treat the area with antibiotic ointment.

I didn't have any.

> Then apply bandages firmly to prevent slipping, but not tight enough to cut off circulation. Keep bandages smooth. Each wrap should overlap the previous one by two-thirds, with the edges parallel. Tuck in the ends below the last layer and secure with a pin or adhesive tape. Never join bandages with knots. Anchor separate strips by binding over a previous layer. Always tie finishing knots on the uninjured side of the limb.

The trauma kit had all the dressing and bandages I needed. After I finished I said, "All done. I'll grab you some clean socks and you'll be fine, but you should try to keep off it as much as possible. Are there any supplies downstairs you want me to go down and grab?"

"Supplies? No. I didn't live there. It was just a safe place to crash. So much for that. Everything I own is either on my back or on my hip." She had a full book bag, and she motioned to a hatchet and a revolver on her hip.

"Wait. You have a firearm. You must be from outside the compound!" I exclaimed.

"How could you possibly know that?"

"Firearms weren't allowed in the housing agreement."

"Well that explains why I haven't found any ammo in this place. Don't get any ideas about shooting our way out of here. I've only got one round left."

I interrupted. "So, how did you get in?"

"Never mind how I got in."

"But it might be a way out."

"I said never mind!" She paused. "I don't want to talk about it, and we're not getting out that way anyway. Besides, what's wrong with the front gate?"

"It's jammed."

"Well unjam it."

"It's not that simple. We're better off finding a good place to climb the wall. Let's just grab my gear and get to the roof. We'll camp up there tonight so you can rest, and figure something out in the morning."

"Thank you" She paused. "My name is Ellie."

Twenty One: Inventory

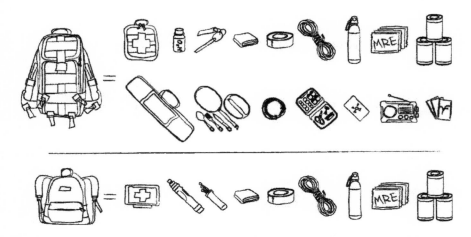

Ellie and I began packing my survival gear bag and her book bag with the most important supplies.

"The idea is to make sure there's redundancy in our packs, in case we get separated." I told her. "I've got the trauma kit, so you take the first aid kit. I'll take the water tablets and the flint lighter. You take the water filter and the matches. Get it?"

"That's actually pretty smart," she admitted. We each took an emergency blanket, a roll of duct tape, and a bundle of paracord.

We were seriously short on water. Between us, we only had a couple of bottles, so I packed both canned food and dry food in each pack.

I had a small tent that I'd never used. It was only meant for one person, but it was compact and fit in my bag. I also grabbed a stainless steel mess kit for cooking, and most of the small gear, the snare wire, the sewing kit, the signal mirror, the solar crank radio, and three packs of Mr. Romero's tomato seeds. They won't be useful on the road, but I'd need to grow food if I ever made it to the cabin.

My pack was almost filled to capacity, and about all the weight I could carry.

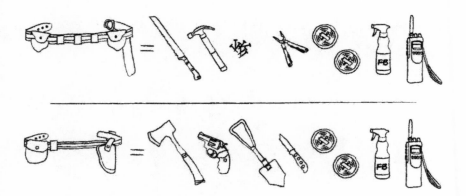

I handed Ellie my CB radio, and I attached Dad's to my utility belt. "Take this. That way if we need to split up we can communicate over great distances, and I can find you." I explained the workings of the radio to Ellie, as Dad had explained them to me.

My utility belt was still stocked with the bread knife, the hammer and nails, and the multi-tool. Ellie's belt held her hatchet and revolver. The tri-fold shovel, and the lock blade each came with their own pouches, so we added those to her belt.

I went around to the other units and collected the rest of the smoke detectors. Using some of the remaining matches I made four more sound bombs.

I had my poncho and she had her hoodie. I set up sludge jugs for both of us. I wore my spaghetti strainer with the LED headlamp, but Ellie didn't want a helmet. She did take Mr. Romero's gardening gloves. Finally, I made a paracord necklace for the whistle, and the compass.

I was testing the weight of each pack when I heard Ellie cry out from another room. I checked and she wasn't in the apartment. In a panic, I ran through Mr. Romero's place, and then the Coopers' place. I found her in Karen's room reading Karen's diary.

"It's all soccer practice, pep rallies, and school spirit. Is that all this girl thought about?"

I stood there, out of breath, heart pounding, but she was calm. "She was an artist... and you shouldn't be reading that."

"I don't think it minds... you know you're in here. Don't you want to know what it says?"

I couldn't answer.

"What? Are you in love with her or something?" she asked in a mocking tone.

"What? No! It's just not yours." I took the diary and put it back on the nightstand. "These are her private thoughts."

"Fine. So, are you the one who tied it up like this?" She pointed at Karen thrashing about in the bed. "What's the point of that? Why didn't you put it down?"

"Why would you kill her? She can't hurt anyone anymore. What if she's still in there? What if there's a cure?"

She laughed. "A cure? You've been stuck in this compound too long. You have no idea what's out there."

She was right. I'd been cut off from the outside world for weeks. "Winter is coming, so if you don't have warm clothes, you should see if you can find something in her closet."

She gave me a look of skepticism. "Isn't that her private property?"

"It's different. She would want us to take what we need to survive."

"Whatever." Ellie began sifting through Karen's closet.

She grabbed a heavy winter coat, complete with faux fur lining. I took Dad's hunting jacket for myself. It was big on me, but it had lots of pockets, and going shooting with him was a memory I didn't want to leave behind.

"I'm almost ready to go. I'll help you get up on the roof, but then I'm going to search the third floor."

"What for? You've got both our bags packed to the gills. What else do you need?"

"Water. We only have enough for a few days, at the most."

"It's not like we're marching into the desert. There's a town less than a day's walk from here, and even if it's completely looted there's a creek right outside."

She was right again. I felt like an idiot. All this time I'd been focused on checklists and book knowledge and it never occurred to me to consider the provisions I'd find on the road. Downtown Thornton would be full of supplies, and there would definitely be game to hunt and trap, and water to drink. The cabin was on a lake. We could purify the water, and fish for food.

"That's a great point. Let's get to the roof."

I helped Ellie up first because of her foot. Stinky was meowing loudly and rubbing against my leg as I boosted her up.

"Don't worry, Stinky. We wouldn't forget you."

I passed Stinky up to her when suddenly it dawned on me. "Just a minute! I forgot the cat food."

I ran into Dad's room to grab what was left of the cat food. As I was doing my last check of the room before bugging out I saw the photo of Mom and Dad holding me at Roger's Campground. I took it, and underneath I spotted Dad's research on the Walking Hunger disease. I took that, too, even though I didn't understand most of it. It was probably the only copy left in existence.

The radio buzzed. It was Ellie.

"Hey! Is this thing on? Hurry up, before you get bit."

"On my way." I packed the cat food, the photo and the research folder in the front pouch of my survival gear bag with my PorcScouts Survival Guide and Dad's zPad.

I took down my distress signal and climbed out of the unit.

Twenty Two: Ellie's Story

The roof was still damp from the rain, and it was dark except for the full moon, which reflected off the surface of the rooftop like a Van Gogh painting.

It was unbearably cold so I started by building a fire. I found an old pallet that I split apart to make firewood, and built a fire pit out of some loose bricks. Then I began preparing a hot meal. I opened a can of clam chowder and added some cayenne pepper I snagged from Mr. Romero's spices. It simmered over the fire as I constructed the tent for Ellie.

It was a one person tent, more or less just a tube with a triangle flap at one end. Barely more than a sleeping bag. Ellie climbed in, lying on her stomach with her head resting on her folded arms.

I brought her a bowl of hot soup, and then without question or prompting she began to tell me her story.

***

We're from Boston, and if you have watched the news you know that Boston is where martial law was first declared. Everyone considered the outbreak a New Hampshire problem until the first reports surfaced in Massachusetts. Then the whole country panicked.

The President went on TV and declared a state of national emergency, and promised to transform Boston into a barricade against the infection. She had no idea what she was talking about.

There were 700,000 people in Boston, and she tried to quarantine us all in our homes. Overnight, they set up roadblocks, and checkpoints. They imposed curfews all over the city.

They started doing house-to-house mandatory medical examinations. They told us the inspectors were from the Health Department, but we knew it was the military.

It was the Roberts family who were the first to resist. Pasha Roberts refused to let in the inspectors. When they rammed his door down, he fired a warning shot into the floor and told them to get off his property.

They opened fire. Mr. Roberts killed four soldiers before they took him out. His wife later said that the inspectors never identified themselves, so he thought they were looters. He was totally justified in defending himself, but no one expected Mr. Roberts and the four dead soldiers to come back. There were no creepers in the house. Why would they? No one knew we were all already infected. That the key to fighting the infection was not to lock away the living, but to properly dispose of the dead. That's how the outbreak got past the barricade.

After that, the army treated every inspection like a potential outbreak. That's when they really amped things up. They sent armored personnel carriers and urban combat battalions down every street. They ordered everyone to turn in their firearms for the safety of the medical inspectors.

All over Boston, people celebrated the crackdown. They even held a pro-military rally in Boston Common, everyone cheering, "USA! USA! USA!" That is, until the military ordered them to disburse on public health grounds. The people worshiped the military. They welcomed them as saviors. But my mom knew better. A lot of people knew better.

No one, not even the patriots, wanted to be disarmed in the panic. Most people just hid their guns away, but a lot of people openly resisted. There was a wave of refusals. People wrote "I am Pasha Roberts" on their doors. Routine medical inspections turned into full military raids. Rebels were declared domestic terrorists.

Lots of people died.

Lots of people came back.

The military was overrun. And the weirdest part was that the creeper soldiers remembered their training. They

98

moved like soldiers. They attacked as a unit. It got to the point that, when you saw a patrol in the street, you didn't know if they were alive or dead. That's when Mom decided it was time to leave.

Most people fled south to stay ahead of the outbreak, but Mom said the outbreak was going to spread everywhere, so there was no sense running. She wanted to find the place where we had the best chance of surviving. So we went north. Smaller population, more guns, and with any luck, the winter would freeze them.

The Air Force was airlifting refugees from infected areas to a FEMA camp in Manchester, New Hampshire. That's how we got north of the barricade. But once we got there we busted out first chance we got. We took all the supplies we could carry, stole a car, and went north. And it was a good thing, too. We heard on the radio that it was overrun like two days later.

We stayed off the main roads and out of populated areas. Everywhere was destroyed. We headed for the White Mountains, trying to get to the snow, trying to find someplace safe. When we found this compound, we both thought we'd finally found someplace we could make a home for ourselves, at least through the winter.

The front gate was hit by a crowd, but we thought we could clear it out, make it safe. We snuck along the wall until we found a large propane tank locked inside a chain-link cage. Mom climbed up onto the cage and pulled me up after her. Then she boosted me up on top of the wall.

I was supposed to pull her up.

The creeper came out of the woods. Just as Mom grabbed my hands, one foot on the wall, ready to leap up, the creeper pulled her other leg out from under her. We didn't see it coming. It ripped her right out of my hands.

***

She was crying.

"Ellie, I'm so sorry. I lost my dad in this mess, too."

She wiped her eyes. "I've been scavenging through these apartments since then, until this Postman thing chased me into this building yesterday. Then all the creepers in the courtyard followed me into the lobby. I barely lost them. I ran up the stairs and hid on the third floor. They went up to the fourth floor. I guess that's when they trashed your place."

"That must be why the lobby doors were left open."

"I tried to sneak out the next morning, but the lobby was still full of creepers, so I barricaded myself inside."

Stinky crawled into the tent with Ellie and burrowed under the blanket with her. They would be plenty warm. I wrapped myself in my emergency blanket and sat by the fire.

"What's wrong with you? I don't bite."

I was puzzled.

"It's stupid to sleep outside in this cold when we'll all be warmer if you just get in here with us... don't worry. I won't tell your girlfriend."

"Just sleep. You need rest more than I do. I need some time to think. We can leave at first light."

Twenty Three: The Dulfersitz Rappel

It was so cold I barely slept at all. Stinky was the first one awake. It was the sound of him thrashing around the rooftop trying to catch birds that woke me up.

By morning, the damp roof was frozen over. Frost covered everything. Winter had come, and soon the snow would come, too. The fire had smoldered out. Breakfast was a cold can of pineapple slices.

I was finished by the time Ellie woke up. She came out of the tent coughing.

"Are you okay?" I asked

"Yeah. The cold is just getting to me. I'll be fine."

"Have some breakfast." I opened a can for her.

While she ate, I stepped up to the edge of the roof and looked down. The PorcScouts Survival Guide had no instructions for this one, but luckily Dad showed me a trick last summer when we went rock climbing. It's called the Dulfersitz Rappel. It's a technique to climb down a cliff with just a rope, and no gear.

The paracord had a test strength of 550 pounds. Both of us combined with all our gear didn't add up to that, and we'd go separately, anyway. Normally I would look for a deeply rooted tree, or a large boulder to anchor to. Instead, I looped the paracord around a large ventilation fan and gave it a good yank. It seemed strong enough. So I tested the length. It had to loop around the anchor by the middle, and both ends had to reach the ground for this to work. It was long enough, but not when it was doubled around the anchor. It was a fifty foot paracord, and it looked like about a forty foot drop. I had to combine both paracords end-to-end, and the PorcScouts Survival Guide had instructions for that.

I flipped to the chapter on knots and it recommended a sheet bend knot which is good for joining the ends of two ropes, even if they have different widths. It's also used in repetition to make a fishing net. The sheet bend is tied by a basic 'rabbit through the hole' method. To be secure, the two free ends of each rope should end up on the same side of the knot, and for extra strength adding another coil makes it a double sheet bend. There were pictures illustrating the different knots step-by-step. I used a double sheet bend.

I looped the new combined paracord around the ventilation fan, twisted the ends together and threw them over the edge. It was more than long enough now.

"Ellie, are you about ready to go?" I shouted over.

"Max! Come listen to this!" She was turning knobs on the solar crank radio, although it played nothing but static.

"Listen to what?" I asked.

"Well, listen to nothing. The emergency broadcast is gone. What does that mean?"

"It probably means the stations lost power." I guessed.

Suddenly, through the static, a voice burst through, "… unconfirmed reports from…"

"Go back!" I exclaimed.

Ellie rolled the dial back, searching in the static, and zeroed in on the signal.

"… using tools, or other higher brain functions." It was Joel Saxen. He was still broadcasting! "Is this some kind of mutation? Are the infected getting smarter?"

Then the familiar voice of Dr. Murphy came through. "I don't think so. I think these aberrations are just statistically rare. Based on my research, we know the disease feeds on the brain of the infected, starting with the frontal cortex."

Joel asked, "And the frontal cortex, that's the intelligent part right? The human part?"

"Yes," she answered, "and the more of it remains intact, the higher functioning they will be."

"How high functioning are we talking about? Could the infected..." Joel's question was drowned out by static.

Dr. Murphy's voice came back. "... haven't seen anything like that, but I suppose it's possible. It depends on variations in the brain structure prior to infection." she answered.

Joel injected, "Prior to infection? You mean healthy people?"

"I mean uninfected people. The disease preserves the amygdala and the hypothalamus. It uses them as a kind of control center. You can think of it as the aggression section of the brain. So, if the disease preserves neural pathways that are wired for aggression, an infected person may retain more brain functions if they're from an aggressive psychoclass."

Joel interrupted, "Wait, what's a psychoclass?"

"It's a mental mode that results from early child rearing. During early brain development adverse experiences or trauma cause physical changes in the brain, specifically an increase in the amygdala and the hypothalamus, which is correlated with increased aggression as adults."

Joel interrupted again, "Are you saying that the more aggressive a person was prior to infection, the smarter they'll be after infection?"

The static swelled and the signal was lost. Ellie tweaked the knobs but the voices didn't return.

"Do you think that explains it?" she asked.

"Explains what?"

"Why the Postman is different. Was he an aggressive person?"

"Maybe. He was a jerk. But we should go. I want to get out of here before it leaves the building. We can try the radio again tomorrow morning. The show probably broadcasts at the same time every day."

We packed all our things, broke down the tent and walked to the paracord hanging over the side. Ellie was still limping from her injury. Stinky followed once he saw we were moving.

"So, what's the plan?" she asked.

"Pretty simple. First, we get off this tower. Then, we find something we can use to climb over the wall."

We stood there looking at the ground four stories down.

"Are you sure you're up for this?" I asked.

"Don't be a wuss. How hard can it be to slide down a rope?"

"I'll go down first so I can show you how to wrap the cord. Watch me."

I set down all my gear, and facing the anchor I straddled the paracord, pulled the tail end around my hip, across my chest, and over my shoulder. I fed the tail end around the back of my neck, and down to my arm and held it in my right hand. I held the anchor end in my left hand.

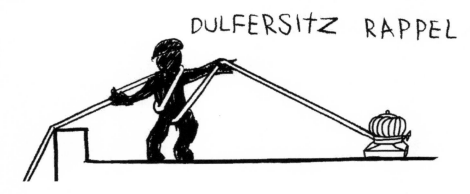

DULFERSITZ RAPPEL

"Are you right handed?" I asked.

"No, left."

"Then you'll want to do this opposite of me."

I rested my weight against the support of the paracord and walked backwards to the edge, feet shoulder width apart, knees bent. Then I leaned back and slowly went over the side. The friction of the rope against my body slowed my descent, and I controlled the speed by gripping the tail end with my right hand. I held the anchor end with my left for balance. It didn't require a lot of strength, just a bit of control. Balance between friction and gravity.

Once I had my footing, I yelled up, "You have to let gravity do the work."

Ellie looked over the edge, and spoke into her radio. "Do you have to yell so loud? Use your radio, Dummy."

Once I was safely at the bottom I said into the radio, "It's all clear down here. Pull the rope back up and lower the gear next."

She buzzed back, "What about Stinky?"

I looked up and saw Stinky looking over the edge. He had a look of recognition. He knew what we were up to.

"I have an idea. Give me a minute." I took off my helmet and tied an end to each handle of the spaghetti strainer. "Pull it back up. I made a basket for him. If you lower him down I'll catch him."

She lowered Stinky, then her book bag, then my survival gear bag. Then it was Ellie's turn.

She wrapped the rope the way I showed her and began her descent. She moved slower than I did, but I couldn't tell if she was having trouble or just being careful of her foot.

She was a bit over half way when she stopped.

"Are you okay?"

Then she let go. Her body fell rapidly. I got beneath to catch her, or more like break her fall. She landed on me and I collapsed to the ground. I was okay.

She blinked awake. "What happened?"

"You fell. I caught you. Sort of." She looked pale, and her skin gave off a terrible heat. I checked her wound and she'd bled through her bandages. There was a nasty discoloration, and it was swollen.

"This looks like an infection. I'm going to give you some ibuprofen to knock down this fever. But we've got to find you some antibiotics as soon as possible." I pressed lightly on her bandage. "Does this hurt?"

She shrieked, and I quickly covered her mouth to muffle the sound. I put my finger to my mouth to shush her and whispered, "Can you walk?"

She nodded and I helped her to her feet.

I spoke softly. "We better move. They built a refugee center at my school. I saw it online. It's a short walk from here, once we're over the wall. Even if it's overrun, there would be medicine there. That's our best option."

"Max, unless this place has an escalator, I don't think I can climb the wall."

I looked at her foot. She stood without putting any weight on it. "Looks like we'll have to figure out a way to unjam that gate after all."

"Great, so what's the plan?"

"Come with me. I have an idea."

Twenty Four: Plan B

Her ankle was so bad she had to put one arm over my shoulder to support herself as we walked. It was slow, but I brought her to the landscaping truck. Stinky stayed close by, while scouting the surrounding area.

"What are we doing here?" she asked.

I slapped my palm on the hood of the truck. "Using the cable winch. We're going to drive this thing over to the gate, hook it up, and rip it open. We can drive it all the way to the refugee center if we want."

"Good thinking. Does it run?"

"Let's find out." I opened the cab door and climbed inside. After some rummaging, I found the keys in the ignition. I hopped in the driver's seat and tried to start the truck. I turned the key, but nothing happened. No lights. No clicking. No buzzing. No choking. No stuttering. Just dead.

"No good." I pounded the dashboard in frustration. "It's got no juice."

"Can we jump it?" she asked.

"No time to search for a working battery. We have to take care of that infection as soon as possible. You could lose your leg, or worse."

"So, what's plan B?"

I went around to the front of the truck and examined the cable, twenty-five feet of quarter inch diameter braided steel with a safety hook at one end. It would hold 1,500 pounds at least. I pulled the cable all the way out, coiling it around my arm as I went. At the other end was a loop, threaded through a hole and secured to the spindle with a bolt.

"I have another idea." I didn't have a proper wrench, but I grabbed the bolt with the pliers on my multi-tool and turned. "Damn! This isn't going to work. I stripped the bolt."

"Let me try." Ellie chomped down on the bolt with a pair of bolt cutters. "Right tool for the job."

"Where did you get those?" I asked.

"From the back of the truck. I think I'll hold onto these."

I unspooled the cable and threw the coil over my shoulder. "Almost done. We just need one more thing. Come with me."

She put her arm over my shoulders again, and we walked over to the tennis courts. There were two nets, each twenty-seven feet long and three feet high. I untied them both from their posts and rolled them up.

"That's everything we need. Let's get to the front gate."

With the cable and netting slung over one shoulder, Ellie on the other, and Stinky following close behind, I led us all to the front gate. I dropped the cable and the nets in front of Sam's booth and looked around for an open car. I spotted a little economy vehicle that someone abandoned halfway through loading. *Perfect!*

"I need your help moving that car over there." I pointed to the rear entry of the south tower directly across from the front gate. "I can set up the rest myself."

"Max, I can barely walk. What makes you think I can push cars around?"

"I don't need you to push. I just need you to steer." I helped Ellie into the front seat, and checked for keys, just in case. "Put it in neutral and steer while I push."

"Will you tell me what the plan is already?"

"Sure, but we've got to be ready when the Postman and its gang comes out of the lobby."

Twenty Five: Many Hands

The courtyard was empty, and all the creepers were in the lobby of the east tower. I crawled through the bushes until I could see the open doors of my building and the mob inside. At any moment, the Postman would come out those doors, the mob would follow it, and everything was in place and ready for them. I just had to wait.

Around midday, the Postman emerged and began walking across the courtyard toward the west tower. The mob lumbered out right behind it, thirty at least, but Ellie exaggerated when she said a hundred.

I was already liberally doused with air freshener, all my gear was safely hidden with Ellie and Stinky near the front gate, and I was hidden in the bushes. The Postman and the mob walked right by me. Their awful stench filled the air as they passed. Their rotten feet landed just inches from my nose as they maneuvered around the bushes I was hiding under.

Just as the Postman reached the entrance to the west tower, I popped out of the bushes in the center of the courtyard, blowing long loud bursts into my emergency whistle. The sharp tone reverberated throughout the complex as the mob turned toward its source. When they saw me, they turned like a school of piranha and left the Postman behind.

I sprinted toward the south tower where the door was already propped open for me.

The floor in the lobby was slathered with rancid tomato sludge, and I was ready for it. I ran and slid in a surfer's stance all the way through the building to the rear exit. I stood in the doorway, sounding the whistle until the mob came into the lobby. I watched as they slipped, falling all over one another.

"Watch your step, you pus factories. I've got more in store for you!"

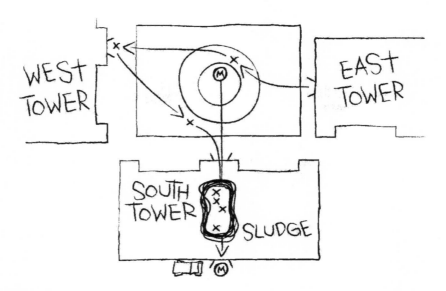

With the mob sufficiently preoccupied, I ran out and hid behind a car Ellie and I had placed next to the rear exit of the south tower, directly facing the front gate of the compound. This left a straight path from the south tower to the front gate.

A few moments later the Postman and the mob spilled out of the building.

"Over here, you parasites. You disgusting wastes of skin! Come get your free lunch!" Ellie's voice called them toward the gate.

The mob charged toward the gate, but when they got there they didn't find her.

"What's the matter, you brain dead freaks?" she taunted.

I watched the Postman pick up the radio we placed at the gate. A confused look covered its face as the mob crowded around.

"Don't you know a trap when you see one?"

Ellie yanked the paracord, safely from her hiding place behind the security booth, springing the trap.

I had attached the two tennis nets top to bottom, woven together through the middle with the steel cable. Then I hooked each end to the gate, making a huge six foot high, twenty-five foot wide snare.

Ellie's paracord ran from the roof of the maintenance building to the roof of the security booth, and when she pulled it tight it lifted our makeshift snare up around the mob, the tennis nets holding them in, and the cable tethering them to the gate.

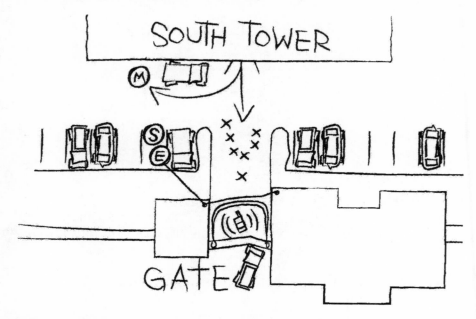

I immediately leapt from my hiding place, blowing my whistle in short, high bursts.

The Postman spotted me and charged, tangling itself in the net. Its grasping fingers jutted through the openings in the net string, and the steel cable pulled tight under its arms, across its chest. The other creepers piled on right behind it, pressing their weight against the trap.

The gate began to creak under the pressure, letting out the signature groans of metal under stress.

Once I had their attention I stopped the whistling and taunted them directly. "Come on. You can do it. You know you want a taste of this." I did a little dance just inches from their grasp to get them really riled up.

One side of the gate ripped away from the security booth and they all lurched forward. I stumbled back and fell on my butt, scrambling away, but they were still tethered. I got back to my feet.

"Is that the best you got? You'll have to do better than that!"

Suddenly the concrete wall of the maintenance building cracked and crumbled as the rest of the gate ripped free. The gate fell over and the frenzied mob began dragging it toward me. The sound of the iron scraping concrete let out a screech so loud I thought my ears would bleed.

I laughed and clapped my hands. "Alright! Come and get it!" And I ran back into the south tower. "Come on. Come on!"

The mob followed me into the lobby, dragging the fallen gate with them, except the gate wouldn't fit through the double doors. It snagged when the bottom hit the door frame, and with just a little more tugging, they yanked it back upright, and it slammed against the outside wall.

That was my queue to retreat. I trudged back through the ketchup and ran around the outside of the tower, back to the car. I pushed the car in front of the door, wedging the gate against the building.

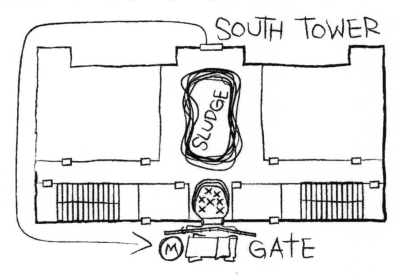

Ellie came out of her hiding place holding Stinky. "Let's see them pound their way out of that one."

I ran to the open gateway. "Check it out! The Postman dropped the radio!" I held the radio in the air triumphantly. "Now, let's get out of here!"

Then something grabbed me from behind. A creeper from the outside attracted by the noise. I screamed as I fell forward. My attacker landed on top of me, and planted a bite on the back of my shoulder. Luckily, it didn't penetrate the reinforced poncho.

I rolled onto my back, knocking the creeper off of me, but it immediately dove after me. It was a thin woman, but strong.

I struggled on the ground with it for several seconds. It very nearly bit into my exposed neck, but I managed to get my hands on its throat and push its head away. Its wet blonde hair whipped me in the face as it shook.

A gunshot rang out, echoing off the distant mountains, and the creeper fell limp on top of me. I rolled it off of me. The woman was wearing a FEMA rucksack, and had Ellie's green eyes.

I looked up and Ellie dropped her revolver on the pavement. Her eyes were welling up with tears, and she fell to her knees.

I picked up the revolver and helped her back up to her feet. "She's your mom, isn't she?"

"No" She wiped her eyes and took the rucksack off the woman. "It's the water we need. Now let's get out of here."

"Good idea." She looked about ready to pass out. "Stinky, you, too!" I patted my leg and he came galloping toward us.

Ellie grabbed my shoulder and pulled me close. She took my hand and placed her hatchet in it. "Now, show me this school of yours."

End Part I

Part II: School Bites

Eleven-year-old Max has escaped the high walls of Lochshire Estates joined by a new companion, a girl named Ellie. Now they must venture through the plague-infested world outside. Armed with only his Porcupine Scouts training, a pack of survival gear, and his determination, Max is desperate to find the medicine he needs to save his new friend. Instead he finds a wasteland of empty houses crawling with flesh-eating "creepers" that stalk the living to satisfy their appetite for fresh meat.

After a chance encounter at his former school, Max is taken into custody against his will. Has he finally found the safe haven he's been looking for? Have they found the community and security they need to rebuild long-term? Or will he discover that school bites?

Part III: Trigger Warnings

Twelve-year-old Max has escaped the smouldering ashes of Thornton Middle School with Ellie and their new friends, Niles and Scott. But now they are being hunted by a vengeful sheriff, and a heartless scientist. They take refuge in Max's lake cabin with another group of young survivors, and must find a way to coexist. After discovering an encrypted signal from a network of pirate radio broadcasters, they discover there are more communities of survivors than they imagined, including some familiar faces Max thought he'd never see again.

Survivor Max: Coloring Book

A collection of the best illustrations from the first trilogy.

SurvivorMax.com

Made in the USA
Columbia, SC
08 July 2021